I0682965

Water under the Bridge

Bridge

Sherryl D. Hancock

PRESS

Published by Vulpine Press in the United Kingdom in 2017

ISBN 978-1-83919-240-1

Cover by Armend Meha
Cover photo credit: Tirzah D. Hancock

www.vulpine-press.com

Acknowledgements

As always, thank you to my beautiful wife Tirzah who is my life and love and who is responsible for helping me bring these stories to life for all of you to read.

Thank you too, for the people who are willing to read a new author, and give me a chance to be heard. I am forever humbled by your kind acceptance.

For lovers everywhere who need to believe that everything happens for a reason and that their love is strong enough to survive anything. Keep believing, it's worth every second!

Chapter 1

"What're you doin'?" Tyler Hancock asked her wife as soon as she picked up her call.

Air Force Captain Shenin Devereaux-Hancock smiled; it was something Tyler had always said as a greeting when she knew who was calling.

"Driving in fun LA traffic, how about you?" Shenin replied.

Tyler sat back in her chair in her office on base, putting her combat-booted feet up on her desk and smiling.

"Just kicking back and relaxing for the next few minutes," Tyler replied.

"And then what?" Shenin asked, knowing that Tyler rarely relaxed for long when she was on duty.

"Oh, Obama is expected to come through, so we're on," Tyler said mildly.

"Brat!" Shenin said, scowling. "Ask him for that transfer while you've got his ear."

Tyler chuckled. "Yeah, that'll be the first thing I say to him, 'Hey Mr. President, I know you're busy dealing with national issues, but can you sign this transfer request so I can go be with my wife in California?' That'll go over big."

"Hey, he's married and in love with his wife, I think he'd understand…" Shenin said, her tone reflecting the grin on her face.

"Yeah, yeah…" Tyler said, smiling at her end too. "So what does your day look like?"

"Oh, the usual chaos. It's astounding how many of these units need aviation resources. I feel like I'm constantly juggling," Shenin said, shaking her head.

"Well, you got into this because you're good at logistics," Tyler pointed out.

"I got into this because that last accident really trashed my ability to do security force work," Shenin said, scowling.

"Okay, but you're good at what you do now, babe…" Tyler said, sensing her wife's mood drop from over twenty-six hundred miles away.

Shenin was silent on the other end of the phone.

"Shen…" Tyler queried, her tone worried.

Shenin blew her breath out, knowing that worrying Tyler wasn't going to help anything.

"I'm here, I'm fine," she replied, almost automatically.

Tyler sensed that as well. Pressing her lips together she fought the anger that rose every time Shenin put her off. Shenin Devereaux was the only woman Tyler had ever loved to the point of feeling complete. Unfortunately, loving someone that much meant that you felt every nuance of their moods, good or bad, and that wasn't always helpful. Loving someone as headstrong as Shenin Devereaux also meant having to try and work around her stubborn nature that kept her from asking for help when she needed it.

"So, how is it going at the department itself?" Tyler asked, purposely lightening her tone.

"Okay," Shenin said, shrugging at her end.

"Making any friends?" Tyler asked, knowing that Shenin was a social person. She needed to have people to talk to; that would help her settle in better.

Shenin had been in Los Angeles for eight months, six of which had been with her new assignment as the Air Force Aviation Liaison to the Department of Justice's LA IMPACT task force. It was very different from their lives in Washington, D.C. where Tyler was part of the security force at Andrews Air Force Base, and Shenin had been a logistics officer. They had Tyler's family in Maryland, a lot of family, as well as friends they'd made over the almost four years they'd been married. Now Shenin was alone in a different city.

"A couple," Shenin said, her tone taking on an edge.

"Uh... Why that tone?" Tyler asked.

Shenin cleared her throat, also knowing her wife quite well. "They're lesbians," she said.

"Uh-huh..." Tyler murmured, knowing that wasn't the part Shenin was worried about telling her.

"They're both involved. I mean, Skyler's even married, but Jet has a girlfriend."

"Skyler and Jet?" Tyler repeated, like she was making a list.

"Stop it," Shenin countered immediately.

"What?" Tyler asked, grinning.

"You know what," Shenin replied.

"They're butch, huh?" Tyler asked.

Shenin didn't answer for a moment, her eyes narrowing on her end of the phone. Finally she sighed. "Yeah, they are. So?"

Tyler shook her head on her end; she knew that Shenin hadn't wanted to tell her that part.

"Why do you assume I have a problem with them because they're butch?" Tyler asked, her blue eyes sparkling with heat.

"I know how you get," Shenin told her.

"How I get?"

"How you think."

"And how do I think?"

"You think that because they're butch they'll hit on me," Shenin said.

"That does tend to be the pattern," Tyler said.

"With me or with lesbians?" Shenin asked, narrowing her gold eyes.

"With butch lesbians hanging out around a very femme lesbian who happens to be very hot, and with no wife in evidence," Tyler replied, her tone heated.

"And if they hit on me, naturally I'm just going to go to bed with one of them, right?" Shenin asked, her tone reflecting her annoyance at the direction of the conversation.

Tyler blew her breath out; this wasn't the conversation she'd wanted to have either. She couldn't help her reaction when she heard about other women around her wife. Without a doubt, Shenin was one of the most beautiful woman she'd ever come across. Tyler knew that lesbians, attached or not, tended to flirt. Right now, that was the last thing Tyler wanted to think about with Shenin on the other side of the country.

"Ty?" Shenin queried when Tyler didn't answer.

"Babe, it's not that, okay?" Tyler said, putting her feet on the floor in her desire to fix the conversation.

"It is that, Ty," Shenin said, her voice serious.

Tyler closed her eyes at her end of the line, knowing she'd just pissed her wife off and also knowing that nothing she could say right then was going to fix it.

"I gotta go," Shenin said then, wanting to get off the phone.

"Shen…" Tyler began.

"Don't," Shenin said shortly. "I gotta go."

With that Shenin hung up.

At Andrews Air Force Base in D.C., Tyler threw her phone across the room.

"Goddamn it!" she yelled.

She absolutely hated the distance between them, and what was really eating at her was that it wasn't just miles. There was an emotional distance between them, and Tyler couldn't seem to get through to bridge that distance. The eight months on the other side of the country hadn't helped at all. Tyler hadn't even been able to get out to California since Shenin had been transferred. It was driving her crazy. Things at the base had been insane, taking up so much of Tyler's time that she barely had time to eat or sleep, let alone have a relationship with her wife. Tyler knew that it wasn't the only thing causing problems though, Shenin had been distant since the incident.

Tyler hated to even think about that time the year before. There'd been a mission to establish a small operation in Iraq near Baghdad. For once Shenin and Tyler were scheduled for the same mission. Shenin was the operational logistics officer and Tyler was part of the security force. However, at the last minute, Tyler had gotten pulled from the mission and Shenin had gone to Baghdad without her. The entire team had been captured by ISIS members. It had been a terrifying month that Tyler simply remembered as a nightmare. Shenin had finally been returned, wounded, but alive. The distance between them had been growing since that time.

In Los Angles, Shenin got to the office, and got out of her car. She stood smoking for a few minutes, doing her best to calm her nerves. She was still out there when Jet's black Maserati pulled into the lot. Shenin looked over and once again found herself astounded by the outrageously expensive car.

The day after the division-wide meeting where Shenin had introduced herself and the program she worked for, she met Jet Mathews for first time. Shenin was in the parking lot getting her gear bag out of the rental car she was driving and was struggling with it because it was stuck on something in the car. Jet drove up and getting out of her car, she immediately offered assistance.

"I got that," Jet said, seeing the problem and reaching past Shenin to pull aside the strap that was getting caught under the seat.

"Thanks," Shenin said, moving to take the gear bag.

Jet held the bag fast, her light green eyes sparkling. "We're going the same way, I'll take it."

Shenin looked back at the woman, naturally sensing that she was gay. Jet had a very butch look about her, but that alone wouldn't have been a tip off. The fact that Jet's eye contact was direct, and held a few seconds longer than necessary, was the tip off.

"Okay," Shenin agreed, then her eyes settled on the car that Jet had parked in the space next to Shenin's. "Holy crap, is that a Mas?" she asked.

Jet grinned widely, inclining her head. "Yep."

"Nice…" Shenin said, nodding.

They became fast friends.

"Good morning?" Jet asked, walking over to Shenin. She could see that Shenin had obviously been standing there smoking for a bit, since there were a few butts on the ground.

"Sure, if you say so," Shenin replied, her eyes slightly narrowed.

"Uh-oh," Jet said, grinning as she pulled out a cigarette to join her friend. "What happened?"

Shenin shook her head. "Nothing, just not a good morning so far," she said.

Jet narrowed her eyes. Shenin was normally fairly cheerful, even in the morning, so this was odd enough to pursue.

"Come on…" Jet cajoled. "You can tell me."

Shenin looked back at Jet for a long moment. In her head she was doing the math; she could definitely understand Tyler's concern if she'd actually seen Jet Mathews. Jet was beyond handsome. She had black hair that was worn loose and shaggy down to her collar, with really beautiful light green eyes and a long leanly muscled frame. Then again, so was Skyler Boché, who actually looked a lot like Jet, with shorter dark brown hair and light blue-green eyes. She was a little more strongly built too. Yes, the two women she'd become friends with were quite attractive, but Tyler didn't know that. All she knew was that they were butch, and that's what pissed Shenin off.

"What if I don't want to tell you?" Shenin asked, her grin wry.

"You know you do," Jet said, grinning.

"Do I now?" Shenin countered.

Jet gave that brilliant white smile, which would definitely have lesbians all over LA checking up to see what their wives were up to at that moment.

"Don't give me that smile, Jet Mathews..." Shenin said, narrowing her eyes.

"Who's doing what to who?" Skyler asked as she walked up to the two, her grin wide as she looked between them.

"Jet's trying to charm me," Shenin said, waving her hand in Jet's direction.

"She can't help that, it's a habit," Skyler said, winking at Jet. "So what's up?"

Shenin rolled her eyes, dropping her cigarette and stubbing it out with a sandaled foot. She was dressed in civilian clothes that day. She only wore her Air Force uniform when she knew she was going to the base.

Blowing her breath out, she saw that both women were now looking at her expectantly.

"Jesus, you two are like bookends!" Shenin said, moving to grab her gear bag.

Jet and Skyler exchanged a look, grinning at the analogy. Skyler moved to take the gear bag from Shenin.

"I got it!" Shenin insisted.

"Uh-huh," Skyler said, as she took the bag out of Shenin's hand and shouldered it.

"See? This kind of thing is what's going to drive Ty nuts…" Shenin said, then grimaced as both Jet and Skyler turned to look at her.

"Whoa… Okay, where did that come from?" Jet asked, raising a black eyebrow.

Shenin sighed and leaned against her car.

"I told Ty about you two this morning and she got all pissed off."

"Wait, you hadn't told her about us before now?" Skyler asked, setting the gear bag on the car's roof.

Shenin shrugged. "It never came up before."

Jet and Skyler exchanged a look.

"So, you told her about us this morning?" Jet asked.

"Yeah," Shenin said. "She asked if I was making any friends here."

"And you said that the two friends you've made here are butch?" Skyler asked looking surprised.

"Well, I didn't say, 'yeah I made friends with the two hottest butches in the department', geeze!"

Jet and Skyler both chuckled at the inference.

"But you obviously told her that we're both butch," Jet said.

9

"Yeah," Shenin said, nodding.

"And you only told her today because she asked?" Jet asked.

"Yeah…" Shenin said, her voice trailing off as she saw the look of *oh Jesus* on Jet's face. "Why?"

"And she got pissed," Skyler said.

Both Skyler and Jet had seen pictures of Tyler. With the exception of the long golden brown curly hair, Tyler was very butch. They knew what the problem was immediately.

"Yes, she got pissed, and that's not okay with me," Shenin said.

"Why?" Jet asked.

"What do you mean why?" Shenin asked, her look baffled.

"Are you trying to tell us that you didn't know she'd react like that?" Skyler asked.

Shenin sighed, rolling her eyes heavenward. "I'm trying to tell you that it's bullshit that she acts like this at all. I've never given her a reason not to trust me."

"Dev…" Jet said, shaking her head. "She's away from her girl. That's bad enough, but to know that her girl is making friends with butches that she doesn't know from Eve…" Jet's voice trailed off as she grimaced.

"What's the big deal?" Shenin asked. "I even told her that you two were both involved with women."

"Won't matter," Skyler said. "She doesn't know us so she won't trust us."

Shenin made a 'pfft' sound. "It's stupid."

Jet grinned. "It may be, but I can't say I blame her."

"Nope," Skyler confirmed.

Shenin looked between the two of them befuddled. "Why?"

"Well," Jet said, "for one, you're pretty hot, Dev."

"Yeah, no one could miss that," Skyler said, shrugging.

"And like I said, she's way over there, and you're here," Jet said.

"Well, that's not my fault," Shenin said defensively.

"Is it her fault?" Skyler asked, knowing the answer, because Shenin had told them why Tyler was still back in Washington D.C.

"Damnit!" Shenin exclaimed. "No, but she sure as hell could have come out here by now to meet you two, right?"

"You mean the two butches she knew nothing about until this morning?" Jet asked, her look amused.

"Oh, shut the fuck up, Jet!" Shenin growled, even as she started to grin.

Jet chuckled. "If you were my girl, I'd be pretty paranoid too," she told her.

"I second that," Skyler said, nodding.

"You aren't going to tell Ty that when you meet her, are you?" Shenin asked her look wry.

Jet and Skyler both laughed, and the three of them walked into the office together.

***

Sebastian was staring at numbers on his computer screen when he heard the knock on his office door. Looking up, he saw Ashley standing there smiling at him.

"Hi," he said warmly.

"Hi," Ashley said, smiling.

"Glad you could make it," he told her.

"Well, you did say you were going to make it up to me..." Ashley said her look amused.

"I did and I am," Sebastian said, looking at his computer screen again. "Come on in," he said, beckoning with his left hand, while his right hand tapped at the computer keys.

Ashley walked into his office, looking around. She'd never been in there before. She walked over to the wall where pictures and framed certificates hung. She saw pictures of him with a group of men, obviously Army Rangers like him. There were also pictures of him and Kashena Windwalker-Marshal, an ex-Marine.

She knew that Kashena was his best friend, and that they'd been partners in law enforcement since they'd gotten out of the service. As a woman, she'd be threatened by what was obviously a very close association, except that she also knew that Kashena Windwalker-Marshal was gay and married to a woman. Ashley found it endearing that Sebastian was best friends with a lesbian. For all that, he looked like he'd be very macho. He definitely had a soft side when it came to his best friend. Ashley had seen Sebastian with Kashena at Skyler and Devin's wedding six months earlier. It was obvious they knew each other well, and that they were very close. Ashley liked that a lot about Sebastian.

When she turned to look at Sebastian she saw that he was watching her now.

"What?" she asked self-consciously.

"I'll just be a couple of minutes, okay?" he said, his gray-green eyes on her.

"Okay," she said, smiling at him.

At that point a man walked in, his eyes on her appreciatively.

"Did you need something Jacobs?" Sebastian asked, his tone sharp.

"Oh, sorry, sir," the man said, grimacing.

The man walked over, handing Sebastian a piece of paper. Sebastian narrowed his eyes at the man, his look stern. As he read the paper, the man's eyes strayed back over to Ashley who was watching Sebastian with fascination.

"Uh," Sebastian said, setting the paper down, and tapping a part of the wording.

"What?" the man asked, startled, and then looked down at the paper. "Oh shit... Sorry boss."

"Language," Sebastian snapped.

"Sorry," the man grimacing again, he looked at Ashley. "Sorry, ma'am."

Ashely's eyes flickered with mild amusement, she'd heard worse out of Sebastian in more formal situations. She tended to think he was giving the guy a hard time.

"Fix it and bring it back, and it better be in the next five minutes, or you're gonna be out of luck," Sebastian said, looking at the silver watch he wore.

"Yes, sir," the guy said, nodding as he picked up the paper and walked out of the office.

After he left, Ashley gave Sebastian an assessing look.

"What?" he asked, a guilty grin already spreading on his lips.

"Don't 'what?' me," she said, her tone chiding. "You were giving him a hard time."

"Maybe," Sebastian said, grinning.

"You were," Ashley said, canting her head to the right. "Why?"

Sebastian's lips twitched, his eyes sparkling with amusement.

"That's really not an answer," Ashley said.

"I know," Sebastian said, moving to stand.

He stretched and then began to roll his sleeves down to button them at the wrists. Then he reached behind him, picking up his jacket and pulling it on. Ashley watched with appreciation. She had already noticed the shoulder holster he wore and found it outrageously sexy.

It had been six months since their date at Skyler and Devin's wedding. They'd talked on the phone a couple of times, but hadn't managed to schedule another date until a month before, and Sebastian had to cancel at the last minute because a search warrant he'd been waiting for had come through. It had taken that long to reschedule their date.

"Jacobs!" Sebastian yelled, winking at Ashley as he did.

Ashley shook her head, pressing her lips together in amusement.

The man came running in. "Sorry, the printer was out of paper!" he said, furtively glancing at Ashley again.

"Focus, man," Sebastian said.

Sebastian read the paper again, and this time nodded and signed it.

"What's your budget for this?" he asked then.

"Uh," the man stammered.

Sebastian looked back at him, his look quite serious. Then he sighed.

"Pull your numbers together and send them to me," Sebastian said. "If I go over budget again this month, Jericho'll skin me alive, so I need those numbers. Don't make any plans till I have the numbers, Jacobs, I mean it. If I have to pull someone's overtime, it's coming out of your check."

Jacobs looked sufficiently cowed by that and he nodded.

Sebastian looked over at Ashley then, "Ready?" he asked her.

"Yes," Ashley said, grinning as she walked over to join him.

They left the office a few minutes later.

"Would you really take money out of his check?" Ashley asked.

"If I was allowed to do that, yeah," Sebastian said, grinning. "He probably knows I can't, but he also knows I'm serious. So he's more likely to do what I told him."

Ashley nodded, trying to understand how Sebastian's job worked.

She'd learned a few things about law enforcement in the time she'd been in Los Angeles, but she knew there was still a lot she didn't know.

"So you've been over budget?" she asked as they got out to his Hummer.

He opened the passenger door, and held out his hand to help her into the vehicle as he usually did. It was one of the very gallant things she liked about him.

Ashley had originally come to Los Angeles while working on a story for the newspaper she had worked for and had met up with a friend from high school. That friend was Jet Mathews, who she'd always worshipped for her outgoing personality, or so she had thought. She'd found that being around Jet, who was a very gallant butch lesbian, had been a very exciting experience. In the end, she and Jet had ended up in bed together. Ashley was, at that time, married to a man who was far from gallant, or even really very masculine at all. In the end, she had decided to leave her husband. She had known very early on that she had no future with Jet, as Jet tended to keep things very casual with women. That changed when she'd gone back to Iraq to rescue a woman who'd saved her life the when she'd been serving there. Jet was in love with the girl, Fadiyah, and it had made it difficult for Ashley to be fooled anymore that Jet would ever love her.

In the end, Ashley had helped Jet and Fadiyah get together, and then made a point of staying out of the way. Even though she was still living at Jet's house, she did her best to make herself scarce as often as possible.

One of the other things she'd done for herself was to ask Sebastian Bach to be her date for Skyler and Devin's wedding. She'd always found Sebastian extremely handsome with his strong build, sandy blond hair and gray-green eyes the color of a stormy sea. He also had all the gallant qualities that Jet possessed that she'd fallen for. She still wasn't sure if Sebastian was a better option than Jet had been, since he was also known for moving from one woman to the next like Jet. Regardless, she was taking a chance.

If nothing else, it was a good opportunity for her to test her dating powers. Jet was forever telling her that she had a great body and was incredibly beautiful, something that was a huge change from her high school days. Ashley was still trying to adjust to that idea. Dating a man like Sebastian Bach was a way to test that.

"Yeah," Sebastian said, "we've been going gangbusters on a few of these old cases, and they're adding up in man hours."

Ashley nodded. "But it's good that you're clearing up old cases, right?"

Sebastian nodded. "Yeah, but until Jericho sees those numbers, I just look like I'm over spending."

"You can't just tell her?" Ashley asked.

Sebastian grinned. "Yeah, I can tell her all day long, but…"

"But she needs to see the numbers," Ashley said, nodding.

"Right," he said. "So I made a reservation at a place called The Craft, it's supposed to be pretty good."

"Okay," Ashley said, smiling.

They talked about various topics on the drive to the restaurant. She found that he was very intelligent and could speak well about lots of topics. They got into a discussion about politics, and while she found out that he was very hard core Republican about a lot of things, he was also reasonable when she pointed things out.

"I think that people should be held responsible for their actions, it's as simple as that," he said at one point.

"Well, I agree with that, but sometimes people come from situations they can't control."

"Right," he said, nodding. "But they can control how they handle themselves in those situations."

"But don't you think that sometimes people get put into situations where they have a natural reaction and are punished for it?" Ashley asked.

Sebastian looked over at her, narrowing his eyes slightly. She could tell he was considering what she had said.

"I think that it does happen," he said. "But I also think that when offered a chance to change the course of their life, people have to make the right choice."

Ashley looked at him, and saw the tightness in his jaw. "Is that what happened to you?" she asked, her voice soft.

He was looking out the windshield, and he narrowed his eyes, his lips pursed in consideration. Finally he nodded slowly.

"What happened?" she asked him.

"Long story," he said, as he pulled into the restaurant parking lot.

"I got all night," Ashley said, smiling.

He looked over at her, raising an eyebrow. "If we spend all night together honey, it won't be talking about my childhood."

Ashley's eyes widened at his statement and felt her pulse quicken at the thought. Oh lord this man was indeed dangerous.

"What is it that I heard they called you in the Army?" Ashley asked.

Sebastian grinned, rolling his eyes, as he got out of the vehicle and walked around to open her door. Ashley turned, putting her hands on his shoulders and starting to climb out. To her delight, he put his hands to her waist and lifted her slightly to lower her to the ground. She came down right in front of him, and she found herself staring at his lips as she did. When she looked up into his eyes, he grinned.

"Maestro," he said.

"Oh my..." she said, widening her eyes.

He waggled his eyebrows at her, grinning.

"Is that because you're so talented?" she asked him.

He looked considering for a moment, then said, "Sure, let's go with that."

Ashley laughed, as he took her hand in his and turned to lead her toward the restaurant.

Once they were seated, Ashley folded her hands on the table. "Now tell me why they called you Maestro," she said, her eyes sparkling.

"I can't repeat it in a lady's presence."

"Oh my God!" Ashley said, giving him an exasperated look. "I promise not to be offended."

Sebastian curled his lips in a wry grin. "You say that now..."

"I swear!" she said, holding her hand up.

"Why couldn't it just be because of my name?" he asked her.

"Is it?" she asked, her eyes sparkling.

Once again he grinned, shaking his head.

"Then?" Ashley said.

Sebastian sighed. "Kash said it was because I could play women like they were violins."

Ashley's eyes widened. "Wow…" she said. "You're that good, huh?"

Sebastian licked his lips and shrugged, looking away with what Ashley could only call a shy smile.

"Did I embarrass you?" she asked.

He looked back at her. "I don't usually talk about that stuff with women."

"Why?" she asked.

"It's a bit crass," he said, feeling embarrassed.

Ashley looked at him for a long moment, trying to equate the man she'd heard about, with the man sitting with her at the table. She looked around the restaurant, it was a nice place, quiet, elegant, but not fussy. Then she looked back at him, and she could see that he was watching her.

The waitress came up to the table then, her blue eyes all over Sebastian, barely sparing a glance for Ashley.

"Can I get you something to drink?" she asked, smiling sweetly at him.

Sebastian pointedly looked over at Ashley. "Honey, what would you like to drink?" he asked, his voice dripping with affection.

Ashley suppressed her grin. "I'd like a white wine, please," she said, smiling at the waitress and batting her eyelashes.

The waitress blinked a couple of times, but then seemed to recall where she was and wrote down the order. Then she looked at Sebastian again.

"I'll have a beer, something on tap?" he said.

"Domestic or craft?"

"Craft, whatever's good."

"Hefeweizen okay?" she asked.

"Yeah, that works," he said, smiling.

The waitress nodded, and walked away, though not without a lot of hip swishing, Ashley noticed.

"That was pointed," she said, looking over at him.

"She was being rude," Sebastian said simply.

Ashley nodded, once again surprised by his actions that seemed quite contrary to everything she'd heard about him.

"So are you going to tell me about what happened?" she asked, once again her voice gentle.

"I guess I should expect you to follow a story, huh?" he asked, grinning.

"Kind of the reporter in me, yeah," she said, smiling.

"My childhood sucked," he said, his look mild. "It's not really much of a story."

"Will you tell it to me anyway?" she asked.

"Classic story, honey, abusive father, and my mother and little sister to protect," he said, shrugging.

"And you protected them?" she asked.

"When I was old enough to, yeah."

"And how old was that?"

He pressed his lips together. "About eleven."

"Oh my God, Sebastian…" Ashley said, looking pained.

The waitress arrived with their drinks, and Ashley wanted to smack the girl for being in the way.

"Are you ready to order?" she asked.

"Give us a few, will you?" Sebastian asked politely.

After she walked away, Ashley reached over touching his hand. "If this is really hard for you to talk about, I don't want to push you," she said, sounding sympathetic.

Sebastian looked back at her. "It's not exactly date talk," he said, his voice indicating that he felt that he wasn't meeting her level of expectation.

"I don't care about that," Ashley said, shaking her head. "I just don't want to make you uncomfortable."

Sebastian smiled at her. "You don't make me uncomfortable, Ash," he said, his tone warm.

"Good," she said, smiling.

"I'll tell you what," he said. "Let's order and have a nice meal, and if you still want to have this conversation we can do it somewhere else, okay?"

"Okay," she said, nodding.

She liked that he wasn't telling her not to ask him questions. Some part of her knew that he probably didn't want to share this much intimate detail with someone he barely knew, and she knew that she should respect that. There was a part of her that craved a connection with someone, but she was also afraid to let that part have its way. She'd had a connection with Jet, and in the end it had really hurt her that it hadn't been mutual.

They ordered dinner, and had a nice relaxing meal, once again talking about easier topics. After dinner, Sebastian took her hand and walked with her out to his vehicle. They drove for a while, and he ended up taking her to a small café where they had coffee, and talked for hours. It was close to two in the morning when he drove her back to Jet's house.

Sitting outside in his vehicle, Ashley found that she really didn't want the night to end, but she didn't want to seem desperate.

"How's that going?" he asked, gesturing to the house.

Ashley shrugged, knowing exactly what he was referring to without needing to ask.

"It's okay," she said.

Sebastian looked at her for a long minute. "It's tough, huh?" he asked then, seeing right through her words easily.

"Sometimes," she said, her tone sad. "Don't get me wrong, I love Jet and I'm really happy that she's finally got someone she loves."

Sebastian nodded looking sympathetic. "But you wish it was you."

Ashley winced at the words; it was hard hearing it said so plainly. She sighed, then nodded slowly. Sebastian surprised her by reaching out to touch her hand. She looked up at him and she could see the sympathy in his eyes.

"It's okay," she said. "I knew going in with Jet, how she was. I slept with her anyway, and was dumb enough to fall for her. It doesn't mean that love will never happen again."

Sebastian nodded. "True, but it doesn't make it hurt less right now, does it?"

"Not really, no," Ashley said.

Sebastian moved to get out of the vehicle, coming around to her side to open her door. Once again he lifted her out, bringing her down in front of him. This time, however, he lifted his hand to her cheek, and then brought his lips down to hers.

Ashley was surprised and thrilled by the gesture, and further thrilled when his lips moved so confidently against hers. She found herself reaching up to pull him closer, causing him to groan softly against her lips. That sound shot right through her, and she pressed closer to him in response. Their lips met over and over, his arms wrapped tightly around her. Ashley couldn't begin to think about anything other than the sensations his lips were causing inside her. Whereas previously she'd thought maybe she was gay, and that she'd end up with a woman, she found out that evening that she was still very attracted to men, at least this particular man.

When their lips finally parted, both of them were feeling very heated. Regardless, Sebastian took her hand and walked her to Jet's front door. Turning, he touched his finger to her chin, tilting her face up to his and kissed her sweetly on the lips once more. He stood waiting for her to go inside, and then walked back to his vehicle. Once inside, he lit a cigarette and thought of the cold shower he needed to go home and take.

Inside the house, Ashley leaned against the front door, and wanted to scream in joy. If nothing else came of this night, she had learned that a man like Sebastian Bach, could definitely excite her senses like Jet had. Maybe there was hope for her love life after all. She went up to her room and found that she was still quite excited by the kissing. It took a long time to fall asleep that night, but she fell asleep with a smile on her face.

Chapter 2

The first impression Marcel and Todd Mathews got of Fadiyah Antar was her obvious effect on their only child. They had arrived in Los Angeles the night before, and had come to have lunch with their daughter. Their relationship with Jet was at best, acrimonious. Jet rarely, if ever, let them know what was happening in her life. Years before when she'd joined the Army shortly after high school, Todd had done his best to talk his headstrong daughter out of such folly, but Jet hadn't been dissuaded in the slightest. If anything it had made her more determined to follow her own path.

Marcel and Todd were quite well off. Todd was a very successful real estate broker, and Marcel's family had money. They had expected Jet to follow the logical path of college, career, marriage, and children. The first shock had come when their daughter announced to them that she was a lesbian and didn't care what they thought. Later, they found that not only did Jet not intend to settle down and have kids with a man, she didn't seem to want to settle down at all. Every time they asked her about someone in her life, she told them that she didn't have a 'girlfriend.' It was a source of concern for Marcel and Todd; they were worried that their daughter would end up alone.

The extent of Jet's purposeful disconnect from them was extreme at times. She had not informed her parents the first time she'd been deployed to Iraq. The only reason they'd known of her time there originally, was when they'd been informed that she'd been killed in action. A mistake, fortunately, but it had shocked them to the core. It had been the impetus they'd needed to start trying to reach out to their daughter. Their sudden "interest" as Jet coined it, only served to irritate their independent, headstrong daughter even more and she'd pushed them farther away. They'd been attempting to come to visit Jet for months, but every time they would contact her, she would put them off. In some cases Todd's work also got in the way, which usually seemed to relieve Jet more than anything else, much to their dismay.

They had finally managed to schedule time with Jet, and had arrived at the house as arranged, only to find that she wasn't answering the door. Against his better judgment, Todd used his key, when Marcel reminded him sharply that the house did belong to them after all. At their suggestion, Jet was staying in the house as a 'favor' to them. Walking through the house, they heard music coming from the backyard and walked to the back door.

They saw Jet sitting in one of the patio chairs facing to the side; she was smoking and drinking coffee. There was an exotic looking dark haired woman with her and they were talking. But as the song on the stereo changed, the young woman smiled and moved to sit on Jet's lap. Both Marcel and Todd were very surprised when they saw their daughter singing the words to the song, staring up lovingly at the young woman on her lap. It was an enchanting scene, and one they never thought they'd see.

Jet sang the last lines of Fadiyah's favorite song, her hands at the girl's waist, her light green eyes full of emotion.

Fadiyah smiled brilliantly down at Jet. "You know I love that song."

"Of course I do," Jet said, smiling.

"And I love you," Fadiyah said, taking Jet's face in her hands gently.

Jet's hand reached up to touch Fadiyah's cheek and then she drew her face down to hers, kissing Fadiyah's lips softly. When their lips parted, they looked into each other's eyes for a long moment. That's when Jet heard the back slider open. Her head snapped around and she moved to stand, carefully moving Fadiyah off her lap to do so.

"We're sorry if we're interrupting," Marcel said, a strange light in her eyes that Jet saw right away. "You didn't answer the door..."

Jet looked momentarily contrite, but then she narrowed her eyes slightly. "Guess you used your key," she said, her tone even.

"Jet..." Fadiyah said from beside her.

They'd had a lot of conversations about Jet's parents coming to visit and Fadiyah had been bound and determined that Jet would at least give her parents a chance before getting nasty. It was already heading in a bad direction.

Jet closed her eyes for a moment, reaching down to take Fadiyah's hand, squeezing it gently. When she opened her eyes again, they sparkled with amusement. Her parents had no idea what to expect with that particular look in their daughter's eyes.

"Mom, Dad," Jet said, her smile crooked, "this is Fadiyah Antar, my girlfriend. Fadi, these are my parents, Marcel and Todd Mathews."

Marcel and Todd both looked shocked by the term 'girlfriend,' but managed to cover that shock by nodding and smiling at the girl.

"It is very nice to meet you," Fadiyah said, inclining her head respectfully as she would when meeting a man's parents.

"It's lovely to meet you," Marcel said, smiling at Fadiyah.

"Nice to meet you," Todd said, his smile warm.

"Can I get you some coffee?" Fadiyah asked.

Jet held her hand up. "Warning, it's Arabian coffee, and it's strong."

"How strong?" Todd asked, always up for a challenge, especially from his headstrong daughter.

Jet grinned as she picked up her cup from the table, handing it to him. Todd took a drink and did his best to control the wince that followed. Jet grinned, her tongue between her teeth in amusement.

"I'll take some," Todd said, his light blue eyes looking challengingly at Jet's.

Todd handed the cup to Marcel who took one sip and coughed.

"Oh my lord, Jet, how do you drink that stuff?" her mother said, shaking her head, and handing the cup back to Jet.

"Well, when you need to stay awake in the desert in the middle of the night…" Jet said, her tone trailing off ominously.

"I will get you a cup," Fadiyah said to Todd. "Can I get you some tea?" Fadiyah asked Marcel.

"That would be wonderful," Marcel said, smiling.

"Cream and sugar, babe," Jet told Fadiyah, who nodded as she walked inside the house.

"She's lovely, Jet," Marcel said, her eyes shining.

Jet grinned, but nodded. "Yeah, I know," she said. She picked up her cigarette and re-lit it, sitting back down as Todd and Marcel did the same.

When Fadiyah came back out, both Todd and Jet stood. Fadiyah smiled shyly, still ever astounded by Jet's chivalry; it was apparent she'd gotten some of that from her father. She went to hand Todd the cup, and he put his left hand out to take it.

"Dad, no!" Jet said immediately, putting her hand out to stop him.

Todd looked shocked by Jet's sharp order, but he put his hand down and looked at Jet quizzically.

"Use your right hand," Jet said, her tone easier then, her look mild.

"Jet, it is not important," Fadiyah said, as she handed Todd the coffee. He took it with his right hand, still looking confused.

"It is," Jet said, her tone sure. "It's your culture, and if we're all going to be part of your life, we're *all* going to respect that."

"But he did not know," Fadiyah said, her tone reasoning.

Jet nodded. "I know that, and now he does."

Fadiyah gave her a questioning look, but then looked at Todd again.

"It is tradition in my culture to only accept food and drink with the right hand," she told Todd, her voice low and respectful. "It is believed that the left hand is unclean."

"Oh," Todd said, nodding and glancing at Marcel who nodded also. "I didn't know, I apologize."

"It is no worry," Fadiyah said, glancing over at Jet. "Your daughter is very vigilant about my culture."

Todd nodded again, looking at his daughter, and catching the exchange of looks between Jet and Fadiyah. It was obviously something they discussed a lot.

Todd sat down, noting that Jet offered her seat to Fadiyah and moved to sit on the arm of the chair after Fadiyah sat down.

"So where are you from, Fadiyah?" Marcel asked, looking fascinated.

"I am from Iraq," Fadiyah said.

Both Marcel and Todd looked shocked, which caused Jet to grin as she took a long drag off her cigarette.

"Fadiyah is the reason I went back to Iraq last year," Jet told them. "She's the one that saved my life over there."

The shocked looks on both her parents' faces had Jet looking at Fadiyah, her light green eyes twinkling in amusement as she waggled her eyebrows at the girl.

Marcel leaned across Todd, and touched Fadiyah's folded hands with her right hand, her eyes shining with unshed tears.

"Then we owe you a debt," Marcel said, surprising Jet with her sincerity. "Thank you for what you did."

Fadiyah simply smiled, inclining her head. "It was my honor, Jet is an amazing person. I am very lucky to know her."

Both Todd and Marcel were surprised by Fadiyah's declaration, however, they noted that Jet did not seem surprised. In the silence that ensued, Todd looked around at that backyard.

"Well, Jet, this looks remarkable," he said sincerely.

Jet grinned, reaching around Fadiyah's back for another cigarette as she did.

"Let me show you what I'm doing over here," Jet told her father as she got up and lit her cigarette. She leaned down to kiss Fadiyah on the lips before she gestured to her father toward the back part of the property.

As Jet and Todd walked away, Marcel moved to sit in the chair closest to Fadiyah. Jet noted the movement and raised an eyebrow. Fadiyah glanced at her, seeing the raised eyebrow and smiling.

After a few minutes of discussing what Jet was doing in terms of the yard, Todd leaned against a post, looking at his daughter.

"She really is lovely," Todd told Jet. "How long have you two been together?"

Jet looked back at her father, surprised by the question, but knowing that Fadiyah would be mad at her if she didn't try to be nice to her father. So she ignored the urge to make a smart ass comeback.

"About six months," Jet said.

"That's some kind of record for you, isn't it?" Todd asked, grinning.

Jet chuckled. "Well, yeah, stateside, it is."

Todd looked confused. "Stateside?"

Jet cleared her throat, already kicking herself for making that distinction. "I was dating someone in Iraq for two years," she told him.

"Oh," Todd said, nodding looking circumspect.

Jet knew he was dying to ask questions, so she decided to give him what he wanted.

"She was a Blackhawk pilot," Jet said, her tone even. "Her chopper went down, and she was hurt badly. They sent her home, and I didn't see her again for years. Now I work with her here."

31

"And that's not difficult?" Todd asked, looking concerned.

Jet grinned. "Well, she just got married to another woman about six months ago, and she's happy. I'm happy with Fadi, so it works out okay."

Todd nodded, never imagining that his wild daughter had ever formed such close attachments to people. He'd never seen her get attached to anything or anyone for long, with the distinct exception of her maternal grandfather.

"I guess your mother and I really haven't been in the loop with you for years," Todd said, his tone contrite.

"Don't ask, don't tell," Jet said simply.

"Is that how you feel about it?" Todd asked her, surprised by her statement.

Jet nodded. "Pretty much since Grandpa died, yeah."

Todd looked shocked. Jet gave him a surprised look of her own.

"You think I didn't hear all that stuff that you guys said about him?" she asked, her tone taking on an edge.

"Jet…" Todd began, his tone cautious.

The last thing he wanted was to ruin the fragile relationship he was trying to build with his daughter. It was already too late though, he could see Jet's eyes take on the usual glint of cynicism.

"You need to know how shocked your mother was, and that we had no idea that you were…"

"Gay?" Jet snapped, her eyes flashing. "Like him?"

"Honey…" Todd said, shaking his head, his look pleading. "We knew nothing about the gay community then. And your grandfather hid it from the entire family until the very end…"

"He didn't hide it from me," Jet said, her tone strong.

Todd looked surprised. "When did he tell you?"

"When he figured out I was gay too," Jet said, her eyes holding pain she'd never admit to, especially not to him.

Todd grimaced. "We never meant to hurt you, Jet, you need to know that."

Jet nodded, her eyes looking down, her right knee moving in agitation.

"Did you mean to hurt him?" Jet asked, her eyes shining with unshed tears.

Todd was stunned not only by the question, but by the tears in his daughter's eyes. Weakness was never something Jet showed, especially not to her parents. Todd saw a tiny little window of hope and he knew he needed to grab it while he could.

"No, honey, no…" Todd said, his own eyes filling with tears. "We just didn't understand, and we handled everything so badly, and I'm so sorry…"

Reaching out, he touched his hand to Jet's shoulder, pulling her to him to hug her. As he did, he prayed that she wouldn't shove him away as she had years before at her grandfather's funeral. He was elated when she not only didn't push him away, but leaned into him accepting his embrace.

Jet felt years of closely held anger melt away. She wanted to believe her father meant what he said and they hadn't intentionally been so horrible to her grandfather.

"You're dying?" Jet asked in a shocked voice.

"I am," her grandfather, Jeremiah Hannrahan, responded, nodding sadly.

"But why, how?" Jet asked, her mind going in a million directions at once.

Her grandfather was the only one in the family that knew she was gay. He was her ally. He was the one that assured her there was nothing wrong with her. He was also the one that no one knew was gay too.

"I have AIDS," he told her, his tone gentle.

"That disease everyone is getting?" Jet asked, her tone alarmed.

"That plague on the gays," her grandfather said, his green eyes sad.

"I fucking hate that phrase!" Jet snapped.

"Jet Blue Mathews, do not use that language here," her grandfather said, his tone solemn.

They were sitting in a church, but Jet had long since given up on God and all his wisdom. Her grandfather, however, had not.

"I'm sorry, Gramps," Jet said, lowering her eyes.

"I want you to know," Jeremiah said, his look direct, "that I am setting up a trust fund for you."

"I don't want stuff, Gramps, I want you here," Jet said, shaking her head sadly.

"But that is not to be my little love," he said, his tone sad. "So I want to make sure that you are set, and that you won't have to depend on anyone for anything."

"You mean when they find out?" Jet asked, her tone rebellious.

"Yes," Jeremiah said, nodding. "I don't want you to go through what I had to when I broke with my family."

Jet pressed her lips together, not wanting to cry, but feeling like her whole world was coming apart at the seams.

She'd been visiting with her grandfather every summer for years. It had been that summer when he'd told her that she was different. She'd known exactly what he'd been referring to; it was a secret she'd kept to herself, because she wasn't sure how others would take it. Her grandfather had been sure and he'd intimated to her that he too was homosexual so she 'came by it honestly.' In her grandfather, she'd found an ally. Not that he hadn't always been. He was the one to talk sense into her parents when they had no idea what to do with their wild daughter. Both of them being gay just seemed like a sign to her. And now she was losing him. It wasn't fair.

She walked into his house unexpectedly one afternoon, when she was supposed to be out riding. She heard her parents talking to her grandfather. She was at his home in Seattle for a visit, she'd just graduated high school three weeks before.

"We don't want your kind of perversion around our daughter, it's that simple Jeremiah," Todd was saying.

"It is not a perversion," Jeremiah said, sighing. "And you'll only alienate that girl if you keep calling it that, Todd."

"You need to stay out of this, Father!" Marcel exclaimed. "Jet is my only child, and I will not have you filling her head with this nonsense!"

"I am not filling her head with anything, other than the knowledge that she is loved and accepted by me."

"And the idea that you're going to leave that child all that money, what is she going to do with it? You're just encouraging her to run away from us, and you know it!" Marcel yelled, her voice harsh.

"Marcel, darling, you cannot make that child stay where you want her, she is a free spirit, she needs to spread her wings."

"You stay away from Jet!" Todd yelled. "Or I swear, old man, I'll have you committed before you die!"

"Jet will still be who she is, Todd, you cannot change that," Jeremiah had said, his tone still mild.

"We'll see about that!" Todd snapped, storming out of the room and right into Jet's path.

Jet stared at her father defiantly, her feet apart, her hands down at her side in a fighter's stance.

"I'm gay, Dad, just like Gramps and there isn't shit you can do about it!" she screamed at him.

With that she ran out of the house and disappeared for a week. When she returned to her family home, she informed her parents that she'd joined the Army and there wasn't a thing they could do to stop her. Todd had thought because she wasn't yet eighteen he would be able to force the Army to release her, but they said that since she was seventeen and a half and a high school graduate, she was able to sign the documents herself. It was not a happy time.

Later, Jet drove her Maserati to lunch, her parents were in the back seat. They noted how Fadiyah wrapped her hands around Jet's right upper arm, constantly looking over at her. Jet, as usual, had the radio on and sang every word of every song, even the ones in Spanish. A song called "Sound of Silence" came on, it was a remake of an old Simon and Garfunkel song, done by a group named Disturbed. It was a haunting melody and Jet sang the words, her voice clear and to her parents surprise, quite beautiful. Fadiyah stared at Jet in rapt silence. Jet glanced over at Fadiyah a few times while she sang, smiling. It obviously didn't bother her that Fadiyah was watching her the way she was.

This was a completely different woman that they were witnessing in their daughter and it was an amazing transformation. They exchanged a few looks, Todd was also anxious to tell Marcel about their exchange in the backyard. It was exciting for them to see Jet so happy. They knew that it had been their own actions that had pushed their daughter away from them, and so being able to witness the change in Jet now was, to them, a gift.

At lunch they talked about Jet's job.

"But I thought you worked for Los Angeles Police Department," Marcel said, when Jet said that she worked for LA IMPACT.

"Well, technically I still do," Jet said. "IMPACT is a task force run by the Department of Justice. LAPD and LASD contribute officers to it."

"And they 'contributed' you?" her father asked, his look somewhat offended, like the LAPD had gotten rid of his daughter.

"Well," Jet said, grinning at the look on her father's face. "In my case, Kash requested me."

"Kash?" Todd asked.

"Yeah, Kashena Windwalker-Marshal," Jet said, "my boss. She was rebuilding her team and I had the type of experience she was looking for."

"Oh," Todd said, nodding. "And what kind of experience is that?" he asked, never having known what she'd done in the Army.

"Well, I work for COID, which is Covert Operations and Inform-ant Development. My time in the Army as an MIO helped there."

"MIO?" Marcel queried.

"Military Intelligence Officer," Jet said.

"And what does that job do?" Marcel asked.

"Well, I was technically part of the Infantry division, but I basi-cally gathered and analyzed data and information on the enemy and helped them plan offensives. I also developed sources of information, Iraqi, Iranian, German, French."

"How were you able to communicate?" Todd asked.

"Uh," Jet stammered, putting her finger to her eyebrow.

"Jet speaks many languages," Fadiyah inserted when she felt that Jet wasn't going to tell her parents.

"Which ones?" Marcel asked, looking surprised.

"German, French, Spanish, Arabic and some Farsi," Jet said, her tone off-handed.

"Impressive…" Todd said, smiling at his daughter.

Jet shrugged. "I pick stuff up quick," she said simply.

"You always did," Marcel said, smiling proudly.

"Graduated at the top of her class in high school," Todd said. "Although why they didn't make you the valedictorian I have no idea."

"'Cause I said no," Jet told him.

"You what?" Todd countered, looking surprised.

"I said no, Dad. I wasn't interested in making a big speech."

Todd shook his head at his headstrong daughter; most people would be thrilled at the chance to be valedictorian at their high school graduation.

"If it makes you feel better, I didn't make a speech when I graduated Summa Cum Laude with my doctorate in linguistics at Universität Hamburg either," Jet said, grinning.

"Doctorate?" Todd asked, looking shocked.

"Yeah," Jet said, grinning. "Thanks to the Army."

"And Summa Cum Laude on top of that?" Todd asked then.

Jet nodded, grinning still.

Todd shook his head, he wondered if his daughter would ever cease to amaze and surprise him. He'd always known she was extremely intelligent.

"Well, it does make sense," Todd said, exchanging a look with Marcel, then looking at Fadiyah. "Jet tested off the charts in intelligence, with a hundred and fifty-nine IQ at the age of fourteen."

Fadiyah shook her head, not sure what that meant. "That is high?"

"Anything over one forty is considered genius," Jet told Fadiyah, not looking too impressed with herself.

Fadiyah's eyes widened as she looked back at Jet, then she nodded. "I knew you were intelligent."

"Uh-huh," Jet said, grinning.

"Do not do that," Fadiyah said, giving Jet a scornful look.

"What?" Jet asked, her grin still in place.

"Use that charm on me," Fadiyah said.

"I thought you liked my charm," Jet said, smiling now.

"I do, but not when you are not believing me," Fadiyah said, crossing her arms in front of her chest.

Jet leaned in, nuzzling her lips to Fadiyah's temple. "Are you sure?" she asked, her voice soft.

Fadiyah closed her eyes, smiling softly. "Stop that," she said, with absolutely no conviction in her voice.

Jet nuzzled her ear then, and Fadiyah sighed, shaking her head.

"I hate that you can do that so easily," she said.

Jet grinned, glancing at her parents who were watching them with enchanted looks on their faces, then she looked back at Fadiyah.

"At least I only use my powers for good now, instead of evil."

"Oh, I do not know about that," Fadiyah said. "Did you not charm that officer Jenkins into doing your paperwork the other day?"

"Damnit…" Jet said, shaking her head.

"Mmm Hmm," Fadiyah murmured, looking amused.

Jet put her head down on the table, shaking it. Fadiyah reached over and touched her hair, smiling fondly.

Marcel and Todd knew that their daughter had indeed met her match in Fadiyah Antar.

***

It took three days for Tyler to finally get ahold of her wife again. She knew that Shenin was mad about her comments, but she also knew that she wasn't being completely unreasonable.

"Are we okay?" Tyler asked when she got Shenin on the phone again.

She was sitting in their house in Maryland, looking at the pictures from their wedding that were hanging on one wall. Things had been so simple then.

"Are you sure you want all of those on the wall?" Tyler asked, raising an eyebrow at her wife.

"Why not?" Shenin said, giving her a questioning look.

"Just more of my face than I wanna see regularly," Tyler said, making a face.

"Excuse me," Shenin said, moving to take Tyler's face in her hands. "I happen to love this face "

"Well, you're biased," Tyler said.

"Yes, yes I am," Shenin replied, smiling. "Besides we paid all that money for the pictures, we should display them."

"Fine!" Tyler said. "Just tell me where you want them hung and I'll do it."

"Yes, be my good butch and handle that hammer thingy," Shenin said, grinning.

"Hammer thingy, huh?" Tyler repeated.

"Uh-huh..." Shenin said, her eyes sparkling mischievously. *"And when you're done nailing that stuff, you can nail something else..."*

"Oh..." Tyler said, grinning widely.

She loved that Shenin was forever telling her how sexy she thought she was, or referring to her as the "rock star" when it came to sex. Tyler had never felt that she was particularly attractive; sure she'd had a lot of relationships with women, but had always chalked that up to charm and a small lesbian military population. Shenin had been the one to assure her that she was indeed quite attractive and that many considered her a rock star in the lesbian community. Shenin had gone on to explain that many women in the community wanted to be with Tyler and that Shenin felt very lucky to have landed her.

Their story wasn't really typical. Shenin had been straight when they'd met; they had become best friends while working on the same security force team in the Air Force, stationed at Nellis in Las Vegas, Nevada. But spending time with Tyler, Shenin had developed much deeper feelings for this dynamic, beautiful, smart and very gallant woman. It had taken a lot for them to get together, since they'd met during the time of Don't Ask, Don't Tell in the military. On top of that, Shenin had become an officer, before Tyler, and fraternization between enlisted personnel and officers was strictly forbidden. Tyler had been the one to resist the relationship with Shenin. However, when Tyler had been critically injured while on assignment in Iraq at the Balad Air Base, it had been Shenin who had flown a day and a half to get to her in Landstuhl, Germany. It had been Shenin's visit and her statement,

"You better fight for me, I love you more than life itself, and I will not lose you," that had been the catalyst Tyler had held onto during her recovery. In the end, she'd flown to Eielson Air Base in Alaska to be with Shenin and finally gave into the love she had for the woman. They'd been married less than a year later.

Now she was watching this beautiful woman she was married to setting pictures against the wall and shifting them around indecisively. Tyler sat back grinning and admiring her wife's curves, evident in the short bike shorts and snug fitting tank top she wore. It was summer in Maryland which translated to humid and hot. Shenin's red hair set off by the sapphire-blue tank top was longer than it had been before, but it was very sexy and Tyler loved it. Moving to stand, Tyler slid her hands around Shenin's waist, pulling her back against her, lowering her head to nuzzle her neck.

"Are you sure I can't just nail you now?" Tyler asked, her tone husky.

Shenin turned in her arms, looking up at her. "You want to nail me now?" she asked her tone soft.

"I want to nail you all the time," Tyler said, moving to kiss Shenin's lips.

Shenin immediately slid her arms up around Tyler's neck, pressing close to her. Tyler deepened the kiss, and Shenin moaned against her lips. They ended up making love on the couch for the next hour, becoming hot and sweaty in the process.

"Well now we just need to take a shower..." Shenin said, her eyes sparkling in amusement.

"Well, damn..." Tyler said, moving to get up and taking Shenin's hand to help her up off the couch, both of them naked.

They made love in the shower and again in their bed. The pictures didn't get put up until the following weekend when they had time off again.

Staring at the pictures, Tyler remembered that time, only six months into their marriage. She felt a tug at her heart, wanting to believe that nothing had changed between them, but she knew it had and she had no real idea why.

"Shen?" she queried when she realized Shenin hadn't answered her question.

"I just don't like that you automatically think that because my friends are butch women that they're going to make moves on me, Ty," Shenin said.

"I know, I'm sorry," Tyler said.

"They're really great," Shenin said doggedly. "If you ever get out here you'll meet them and you'll see."

Tyler blew her breath out. She knew that her not having managed to get out to California yet, was part of the problem. She'd put in a request for leave and was hoping it would be approved. Unfortunately, in her position, she was critical to many of the missions that occurred with the security force on base, so it was very difficult for her to get leave approved.

"Okay, babe, okay," Tyler said, her tone placating.

"I miss you, Ty," Shenin said then, her voice sad.

"I miss you too, Shen," Tyler said. "I love you."

"I love you too, Ty," Shenin said. "It's just really hard being here by myself, you know?"

"You're not alone, you have Muffit," Tyler said, referring to the dog that Shenin had brought back from Iraq with her.

Shenin grinned, looking down at the scruffy wired hair terrier that lay at her feet.

"She's cute and all," Shenin said, "but she's really a lousy kisser."

"Too much tongue?" Tyler asked.

Shenin laughed, a wonderful sound to Tyler. "Yeah, you got that right."

"Are you doing good with the shelter thing?" Tyler asked then.

"Yeah," Shenin said, nodding. "I'm getting to work with some of the more timid dogs. They are very sweet."

Tyler smiled fondly. Shenin had not only brought back a dog from Iraq, but a desire to work with animals in shelters.

"They're in cages and scared, I want to help them," she'd told Tyler.

It had taken a while for Shenin to find the right fit, but she was finally settling into a volunteer group made up of PTSD sufferers and it seemed to be helping.

Tyler had been worried about Shenin when it came to PTSD, Post-Traumatic Stress Disorder. It had been quite obvious when Shenin had returned from Iraq that she was definitely suffering from PTSD. Her sleeping patterns had been erratic, or non-existent. She would go for days without sleep, and then finally crash sleeping for sometimes up to forty-eight hours. She lost twenty pounds on top of the twenty she'd lost during her time in captivity. Tyler had tried to talk to Shenin about what had happened, but she'd been very vague and didn't want to talk about it.

Shenin had agreed to see a counselor about the PTSD and that had eased Tyler's mind immensely. It had been the counselor's suggestion that Shenin work with animals, since she'd obviously developed a bond with the dog she'd rescued in Iraq.

Lying on the dirt floor of the cell, Shenin came too feeling the pain of the head wound she'd suffered when they'd hit her with the butt of their AK47, not to mention the gunshot wound she had to her arm. Opening her eyes she was surprised to see the kind brown eyes of a dog staring at her through the bars.

"Hi there," she said to the dog, whose tail had started to wag immediately.

It had been the beginning of a month long relationship with the animal she'd named "Muffit" after the robot dog in eighties TV Show Battlestar Galactica. She knew it was silly, but the dog made her time in captivity less terrifying. In the end, when she'd been rescued, she'd grabbed the dog on the way out, insisting on bringing him home with her.

"So what are you up to today?" Tyler asked.

"Going for a ride with the girls," Shenin said, smiling down at Muffit.

"Which girls?" Tyler asked, too quickly, grimacing as she realized that.

"Well, a few of them, actually," Shenin said. "There's a pretty big group of women here who have bikes. There's Jericho, Raine, Quinn,

Jet and of course their girlfriends come too. I figured the Shadow could use a good run."

"That should be fun," Tyler said, wanting to ask who all of those women were, but also not wanting to sound like she was questioning Shenin again.

"Yeah, they're a pretty fun group," Shenin said, nodding.

"Well, once I get my ass out there permanently, hopefully they'll let me ride with you all," Tyler said, grinning.

"Oh, I think that might be possible."

"What kind of bikes do they ride?" Tyler asked.

"Well, Jericho rides a Harley, nice custom job, you'd love it. I'll take pictures of it and send them. Um, Raine rides a Shadow like me, Quinn rides a Harley too, but hers is an Iron eight eighty-three and Jet rides a Ducati."

"Ducati? That's a nice bike..." Tyler said.

"Oh yeah, and it's a Superleggera, so it's really nice."

"She has a Superleggera?" Tyler asked, stunned. "That's like a sixty thousand dollar bike."

Shenin chuckled. "It's still cheaper than the Maserati she drives."

"Jesus, how much does DOJ pay down there?" Tyler asked.

Shenin laughed. "Not that much. Jet said she bought it with a bonus check she got from doing some contract work with the Army."

"Damn, I'm in the wrong friggin' branch," Tyler said, shaking her head.

"Tell me about it!" Shenin said, grinning. "Oh, and that's not counting the sixty-seven Mach Fastback Mustang she has in her garage."

"The girl does know how to play, doesn't she?" Tyler asked, thinking this Jet was some serious player and she didn't want her wife anywhere near her.

"She does seem to love her toys," Shenin said, knowing she was now talking too much about Jet and that Tyler's ire was rising, so she switched subjects.

"Are you going down to mom and dad's for dinner today?" she asked.

Tyler narrowed her eyes at her end of the phone, catching the sudden subject change. "Yeah, they're doing crab," she said, grinning.

"Ugh!" Shenin said at her end.

Tyler chuckled. "I know you won't miss it, but I'm looking forward to picking a few dozen."

"Have at it," Shenin said, shaking her head. "I won't be there to witness it."

Maryland was known for its Chesapeake Blue Crab, but Shenin absolutely abhorred the practice of cooking live crabs in steaming water. She considered it barbaric, which was something that Tyler's large family, who'd grown up crabbing, found endlessly amusing. She'd threatened on many family occasions to 'rescue' a few of the live crabs. It was just another really cute and endearing thing about her wife that Tyler loved. Shenin often referred to the "rending of bones" and the "carnage" when talking about the crab feeds her family liked to have for special occasions.

"I better get going," Shenin said, looking at her watch. "I gotta meet the girls in two hours and I haven't even showered yet this morning."

"Okay," Tyler said, disappointed that they didn't have more time to talk when they were finally getting along for the moment. "I love you."

"Love you too, Ty, have fun at dinner, give everyone my love."

"Will do," Tyler said, smiling.

They hung up a few minutes later. Tyler sat staring at their wedding pictures, wishing things could be as they were then. They'd been so damned happy. She sincerely wished she knew how to fix things, but she really had no clue where to start. It worried her that Shenin was spending so much time with lesbians down in LA, especially butch ones. But she knew that she had to be careful in what she said, she didn't want to put anymore walls up between her and her wife. It really sucked to be in the situation she was in, and she saw no way out of it.

***

Sebastian walked up to Jet s front door and rang the bell. Fadiyah answered the door.

"Sebastian!" Fadiyah exclaimed happily, moving to hug him.

Sebastian hugged the girl, smiling fondly. Pulling back, he looked down at her.

"You look great," he said, his smile warm.

"I am very happy," Fadiyah said nodding. "You are here to pick up Ashley?" she asked then.

"Yes," he said, nodding.

"She and Jet are out in the back. Do you want some coffee?" Fadiyah asked.

"Jet's got that good Arabian stuff, right?" Sebastian asked, grinning.

"Yes," Fadiyah replied, smiling.

"Then hell yes," Sebastian said, nodding.

He walked to the back door looking out. They were sitting across from each other in the backyard. Ashley was dressed in black capris and a mint-green knit shirt that hugged her body attractively, on her feet she wore strappy sandals. Jet was completely casual in black shorts and a tank top. Jet's bare foot was on the chair Ashley sat in; it seemed proprietary. It was the first thing Sebastian noticed and it bugged him.

"You really think it's a good idea?" Ashley asked Jet.

"I think it's a great idea," Jet said, nodding.

They both turned to look at Sebastian when he walked out of the house.

"Hey Baz," Jet said, grinning up at him.

"Morning Jet Fire," he said, using the nickname he'd always used for her, then he looked at Ashley. "Good morning," he said smiling and leaning down to kiss her lightly on the lips.

Ashley smiled brilliantly. "Good morning."

Fadiyah walked out of the house, and Jet moved to stand smiling. Fadiyah handed Sebastian his coffee, making a face at Jet.

"Jet, your back is bothering you. You do not need to stand for me…" she chided.

50

"Habit," Jet said, grinning and gesturing for Fadiyah to sit in the chair she'd just gotten up out of.

"You sit there," Fadiyah said, pointing to the chair. "I am fine."

Jet looked indecisive, but finally nodded when Fadiyah narrowed her silver-gray eyes at her.

"So what are you two up to today?" Jet asked looking between Sebastian and Ashley, as Fadiyah moved to sit on the arm of the chair Jet sat in.

Sebastian looked at Ashley. "Well, I was thinking breakfast and then whatever the lady would like to do."

Ashley smiled up at Sebastian. "I kind of wanted to check out this new flea market opening up in Burbank... If you don't mind?"

"I don't mind," Sebastian said, smiling.

He took a few sips of the coffee, sighing.

"I miss this stuff..." he said, his look dreamy.

"I can get you some," Jet said, smiling. "All ya gotta do is ask."

"I'm asking," Sebastian said, grinning.

"Then you got it," Jet said, grinning back at him.

The four of them talked for a few more minutes, then Sebastian set down the cup, looking at Ashley.

"You ready?" he asked, holding his hand out to her.

Ashley smiled, nodding as she took his hand and stood up.

"You kids have fun," Jet said, her grin wicked.

"Shut up, Jet," Sebastian said his eyes still on Ashley.

Jet simply chuckled. Sebastian and Ashley left then.

Fadiyah moved to sit in the chair that Ashley had just vacated, looking at Jet. She saw that Jet looked somewhat unhappy suddenly.

"What is wrong?" Fadiyah asked.

Jet looked over at her, shaking her head slowly. "I'm just worried about Ash."

"Why?" Fadiyah asked. "I thought you liked Sebastian."

"I do," Jet said, nodding.

"Then why are you worried?" Fadiyah asked.

Jet didn't answer for a long moment, looking pensive. "Well, I'm just not sure she's upgraded here."

"What does that mean?" Fadiyah asked.

"It means I'm afraid she's traded one player for another one."

"What is a *player*?" Fadiyah asked.

Jet grinned at her, Fadiyah was still trying to adjust to American slang, and Jet constantly forgot to explain herself.

"Kind of what I was, babe," she said. When Fadiyah still looked mystified Jet said, "Someone who didn't stay with women for very long."

"Oh," Fadiyah said, nodding. "But you love Ashley."

"I do," Jet said, nodding. "But she needs someone that's in love with her and will be what she needs. I'm not sure Sebastian is a long-term relationship kind of guy."

"Why do you think that?"

"Well, according to Kash, his nickname was Maestro when he was in the Army."

"Maestro?"

"Yeah, 'cause he played women like they were musical instruments... Used them for sex," she explained when she realized she'd used another colloquialism.

"Oh..." Fadiyah said, looking shocked, but then shaking her head. "Sebastian is an honorable man, I cannot believe that he would do that kind of thing."

Jet looked back at Fadiyah for a long minute, then made a sucking sound through her teeth. "Would you believe I did?"

Fadiyah looked back at this woman who she loved so much unable to see her in the way she was describing herself.

"You were a player?" Fadiyah asked, her voice stumbling slightly over the odd term.

Jet chuckled, nodding. "Oh yeah."

Fadiyah nodded. "Ashely did tell me that you did not get serious about women."

Jet nodded. "She was right."

"But you are serious about me?" Fadiyah said, suddenly realizing that she might be wrong about that.

Jet leaned forward, seeing the doubt in Fadiyah's eyes suddenly. She touched Fadiyah's cheek and leaned in to kiss her deeply. After a few minutes, Jet moved to stand, taking Fadiyah's hand and leading her inside. Jet made love to her for hours that morning, ensuring her with her body and her lips that she was indeed hers.

Sebastian and Ashley had breakfast at an outdoor café. When their dishes were cleared away they sat talking, while Sebastian lit a cigarette, leaning back in his chair. He was dressed in jeans, tennis shoes and a black polo shirt with the LA IMPACT logo on it. It was the most casual Ashley had ever seen him dressed. He was definitely a handsome man, and she noticed the women in the restaurant looking at him.

"So," Ashley said, picking up her coffee and taking a sip. "Are you ever going to tell me about your childhood?"

Sebastian grinned, moving to sit forward, putting his elbows on the table and turning his head to look at her.

"You really want to know about it?" Sebastian asked her, his gray-green eyes mild.

"Yes," Ashley said, her smile warm.

Sebastian nodded, his look resigned. "Well, I told you, my dad was abusive… He'd hit whoever got in his way when he was drinking and sometimes when he wasn't. When I was eleven I started being the one to get in his way," he said, shrugging, even as Ashley grimaced. "When I was about fourteen I got a job and starting saving money. I figured I could get my mom and my sister away from him. I saved the money in a big jar under my bed. By the time I was seventeen I had a lot of money shoved in that jar…" He paused to take a sip of his coffee and light another cigarette, his look far away. "One day I came home, and there was my jar, sitting on the coffee table and my dad was sitting behind it."

"Oh God…" Ashley said, her look pained.

Sebastian's eyes looked over at her, he smiled softly at her sympathy.

"He said 'so look what I found in my house.' I told him it was mine, and he said that nothing in his house belonged to me." He shook his head then, his lips pressed together for a moment. "I lost it and ran

54

into the kitchen and grabbed a knife and threatened to slit his throat with it if he didn't give me the money back."

"Oh Sebastian…" Ashley said in a scared whisper.

Sebastian blew his breath out in a short laugh. "Well he called the cops on me, saying that I was trying to steal his money, his 'life savings' was how he put it. They arrested me for armed robbery."

"Oh my God!" Ashley exclaimed. "Couldn't you explain?"

Sebastian grinned. "Like they were going to believe me? I had no proof, Ash. I did get lucky though, one of the arresting officers knew about my dad, and knew our situation. He suggested that I go into the military, hell, he drove me to the recruiter's office himself."

"That's when you joined the Army?"

"Yep," he said, nodding. "And not too long after boot camp, I was able to move my mom and my sister into military housing with me."

Ashley nodded, smiling.

"So," he said then, leaning back again and looking over at her. "What's your story?"

Ashley smiled self-consciously then. "It's nothing like yours…" she said, her voice trailing off as she shook her head.

"God, I hope not," Sebastian said, grinning.

"It was your average childhood," she said.

"You grew up in Washington, right? With Jet?"

"Well, not *with* Jet, I didn't meet her until high school."

"And how did that happen?" Sebastian asked.

Ashely looked wistful. "I guess you could say she was my rescuer."

"How so?" he asked.

"Well, she was extremely popular in school," she said. "I mean, everyone knew who she was and everyone wanted to be her friend."

"That sounds about right," Sebastian said, his look wry.

Ashley smiled, nodding. "Yeah, she hasn't changed a lot in that respect."

"So you were one of her friends," Sebastian said.

"Well, sort of," Ashley said, looking pensive.

"What does that mean?" Sebastian asked, sensing an undercurrent.

"Well, I wasn't one of the popular people, believe me."

"Hard to believe," Sebastian said, shaking his head.

"Oh, if you saw what I looked like back then, you wouldn't say that," Ashley told him.

"What did you look like?" he asked, curious now.

"I was fat with stringy brown hair and braces," Ashley said, smiling.

Sebastian looked shocked. "You didn't always look like this?" he asked, gesturing to her as a whole.

"Nope," Ashley said. "This took a lot of hard work."

Sebastian nodded, appreciatively. "So where did Jet come in?"

"Well, I'm sure you remember that high school kids are mean to anyone that isn't good looking… Well, maybe you don't."

"Why do you say that?" he asked.

"Well, I tend to think that you were always hot, so I doubt you got teased much."

"Hot, huh?" Sebastian queried, his look amused.

"Very hot," Ashley said, smiling, her look direct.

"Anyway," Sebastian said, his look still amused.

"Anyway," Ashley repeated. "Jet was the one popular person who paid any attention to me. She always said hi to me in the hallways and stuff. Then we went to this horrible camp in our senior year. Jet was amazing, when some stupid girl tripped me the day we got there, it was Jet who helped me up. She then proceeded to pal around with me the entire time. That's when people started being nicer to me."

"And you think that was because of Jet?" Sebastian asked.

"I know it was, Sebastian," Ashley said. "She was like the Pied Piper when it came to friends, and if someone crossed her, they were in Siberia suddenly. That wasn't something I imagined, it was true. Heck, the only reason I ended up meeting her again was because the reunion committee insisted that if Jet Mathews didn't come to the fifteen year reunion, there was no point in having one."

Sebastian looked back at her, shocked by what she was saying. He knew that Jet had a very magnetic personality, he'd liked her the minute he'd met her, but it astounded him that she'd had that much influence as early as high school. It also impressed him that Jet had used her influence obviously for good things, and not to be that mean bitch she could have been so easily.

It jostled against the ire he had with Jet currently. It had bothered him that she'd dismissed Ashley so easily in favor of Fadiyah. Even though he'd been part of the three person team that had gone to Iraq to rescue Fadiyah, he hadn't really realized at the time that Jet was in love with the girl.

She'd been dating Ashley at the time she'd gotten the okay to go back to Iraq. When Fadiyah had been given the choice of staying in Iran, where they'd taken her to after rescuing her quite literally out of the clutches of ISIS members, or going back to America with Jet, she'd chosen to stay with Jet. Sebastian had known that this would displace Ashley, and he also knew by that time that Jet was already in love with Fadiyah. He'd been upset by the turn of events and had been rather vocal about it to Jet. Not that it had made any difference, but it was also what had made such a tender spot for Ashley for him.

"So, this ex-husband..." Sebastian said, turning the conversation in another direction.

Ashley laughed. "Greg," she supplied.

"So, what was the deal with Greg?" Sebastian asked.

"Greg was..." Ashley began, looking thoughtful.

"Was... what?" Sebastian asked.

Ashley sighed. "Greg was the first guy to really notice me when I started to work my butt off to look better."

Sebastian nodded slowly, waiting for her to continue.

She shrugged. "I guess I figured I should grab a good thing while I had the chance."

"And was it a good thing?" Sebastian asked.

"It was okay," Ashley said, "and I thought I was happy."

"But..." Sebastian said.

"But, then I came here and was around Jet."

Sebastian nodded. "And that changed things?"

"I'd say it clarified things for me," Ashley said.

"How?" Sebastian asked.

Ashley shook her head looking thoughtful again. "I guess I really started to see how it felt to have someone treat you like you were really special, you know?"

"Greg didn't treat you like you were special?" Sebastian asked.

"Greg treated me like an afterthought," Ashley said.

Sebastian looked perplexed. "He notices you enough to marry you, and then forgets about you?"

Ashley shrugged. "I guess. I mean, I think he kind of figured he'd caught me so he didn't have to do anything else, you know?"

"Well, that's just stupid." Sebastian said, already intensely disliking Greg.

Ashley smiled. "I didn't realize how different things could feel until I was around Jet."

Sebastian nodded, forcing the jealousy that he was feeling to stay out of his face.

"She's just so dynamic, you know?" Ashley said. "And then one day we were talking about the butch thing—"

"The butch thing?" Sebastian queried.

"Yeah, you know how butch lesbians are versus the femme ones."

Sebastian nodded. "Yeah, okay, I know about that, can't be best friends with a butch for years and not get that. Go on," he said.

"Anyway, that's about the time that Jet made a comment about some men being less masculine than some butches, and that's when I realized that Jet was way more masculine and gallant than my husband was."

"Wow," Sebastian said, his look reflecting his shock and disgust at the same time.

Ashley nodded, understanding his disgust.

"When I went home, I really saw the way Greg was, and I just couldn't stand it anymore, so I left and came back here."

"To be with Jet," Sebastian said.

"No, just to not be with him anymore," Ashley said.

Sebastian nodded, not looking convinced by that.

"I get it," he said. "I was seeing a woman once whose husband was a bit of a wuss. She ended up leaving him too."

"For you?" Ashley asked, raising an eyebrow at him.

"Touché," he said, grinning. "But no, not for me."

"But I can guarantee you, that she wanted to be with you," Ashley said.

"What makes you say that?" Sebastian asked, grinning.

"Because I've met you," Ashley said, her tone wry.

Sebastian laughed at that. "I dunno, I'm no picnic."

"No," Ashley said, grinning. "Probably more like a carnival."

That had him throwing back his head laughing out loud. Ashley found his laugh very sexy, she found everything about the man sexy.

He stood and pulled out his wallet dropping a few bills on the check. He then extended his hand to her.

"Ready to go?" he asked.

"Sure," she said, putting her hand in his and she stood.

She noticed all the envious looks she got from women as they walked through the restaurant to go outside. It felt good to be the woman at Sebastian Bach's side, at least for the moment.

They spent a nice day wandering around a flea market. He had a very warm open way about him that Ashley found very appealing. People responded to him, much like people did Jet, he was very magnetic. Ashley knew that she was likely a fool to be so interested in yet another person that wasn't big on commitment, but she couldn't help but to be drawn to the man.

At the end of the day he drove back to Jet's, once again getting out of the vehicle to open her door and help her down. Ashley put her arms around his neck and kissed him as he lowered her to the ground. His arms wrapped around her immediately as he kissed her back. Once again Ashley felt her body respond to him instantly. He walked her to the door, kissing her softly once more and then left. Ashley was fairly certain she was going to explode soon if he didn't make a move. She watched as he drove away, thinking she was going to need to be a little more aggressive if she was ever going to get this man to do more than kiss her.

Chapter 3

The next day, as Jet zipped around yet another car, cussing at them as she did, Fadiyah looked over at her. She watched as Jet's hand tapped agitatedly and saw that she was singing the music that was on as well. She'd already consumed two cups of coffee and was now drinking a Monster Java energy drink and she was still on edge.

"Perhaps next time we should make the appointment before you run out of Adderall..." Fadiyah commented.

Jet glanced over at her, and grinned. "That's always the plan babe," she said.

"But it did not go that way?" Fadiyah queried, blinking innocently.

Jet laughed. "It never does!" she exclaimed. "Sucky thing about ADHD is you can't remember to make the appointment for the thing that you need to get to take to help you remember."

"How often do you need to go?" Fadiyah asked, pulling out the iPhone that Jet had gotten her a few weeks back.

Marcel and Todd watched from the back seat of the Maserati, interested in how things were going to go in this case. Their daughter was usually quite difficult when it came to being managed or chided for mistakes. So far Jet had shown absolutely no ire toward Fadiyah the entire week they'd been around the couple, it amazed them.

Jet looked over at Fadiyah and grinned. "Are you gonna schedule an appointment to remind me to make the appointment?"

"That is my plan, yes," Fadiyah said, nodding as she opened the calendar function on the phone. She was still getting used to how it worked.

Jet chuckled. "That's cute, babe, but I have a reminder on my calendar. I just forget right after that."

Fadiyah pursed her lips. "Then perhaps I should make the appointment for you."

Jet looked over at her. "Are you taking care of me?" she asked, raising a black eyebrow.

Fadiyah looked over at her, her look considering. "Yes, I am," she said finally, nodding.

Jet smiled softly. "Okay."

Marcel and Todd exchanged a shocked look, their daughter was definitely changing.

Two days later they really saw how much Jet had changed. Jet came home from work early; her back had been bothering her all day so she'd taken part of the day off. When she walked into the house it was eerily quiet. Walking upstairs she looked around and then went into their bedroom. Fadiyah was lying in bed, which was shocking because she was usually up when Jet left.

"Babe..." Jet said softly. She walked over to the bed and reached out to touch Fadiyah's face. "Oh, honey, you're burning up."

She sat down on the bed, looking down at Fadiyah who was shivering.

"What's going on babe?" Jet asked. "What hurts?"

"My… head… and… my stomach," Fadiyah said, her voice hesitant.

"Okay," Jet said, nodding. "Did you take anything?"

Fadiyah shook her head.

"Okay, let's at least get some Tylenol into you for that fever and it might help the headache too… How bad is the pain?"

Fadiyah shrugged.

"Okay, let's say on a scale from one to ten, one being no pain, ten being the worst you've ever felt."

"About five," Fadiyah said then.

"Okay, let me get you some Tylenol," Jet got the medicine and helped Fadiyah sit up to take it.

She then kicked off her boots and removed her holstered weapon. She lay down next to Fadiyah pulling the girl into her arms and holding her. Fadiyah huddled against Jet, her hand grasping at her shirt.

"It's okay, baby girl, I got you…" Jet said, stroking Fadiyah's hair.

They lay that way for a few of hours. At one point Jet heard the doorbell and knew it was her parents, they'd come to take them to dinner. The bell rang a couple of times.

"Use your key, Dad…" Jet muttered.

She heard the key in the door shortly thereafter.

"Jet?" Todd called.

"Upstairs, Dad!" Jet called back.

Todd and Marcel walked into the bedroom a few moments later.

"What's wrong?" Marcel asked, sounding alarmed.

"Fadiyah's not feeling well," Jet said. "We're gonna have to reschedule dinner."

"No problem," Todd said. "Do you want us to stick around though, just in case?"

Jet considered the thought, then nodded. "Yeah, that sounds like a good idea. Thanks."

"We'll be downstairs," Marcel said. He saw the way Jet was holding Fadiyah and felt very moved by it.

An hour later Fadiyah's pain stepped up. She was actually writhing in pain.

"Okay, show me what hurts babe, where does it hurt?" Jet asked patiently.

Fadiyah touched her lower right abdomen.

Jet nodded. "Okay, time to go to the hospital," she said, moving to get up and pulling on her boots.

"Jet, it is okay…" Fadiyah said, shaking her head.

"No, babe, it's not," Jet said. "We need to go. Let's get you dressed."

Jet gently and carefully helped Fadiyah put on a dress that wouldn't bind her stomach and then called down to her father.

"Dad, we need to go to the hospital, we need to use the Range Rover, will you drive?"

"Of course, do you need help?"

"No, I've got her," Jet said, carefully picking Fadiyah up. Fadiyah moaned softly. "I'm sorry babe, I've got you, hold on to my neck, okay?"

Jet carried Fadiyah down the stairs, Marcel waited there with a throw from the couch and was holding the door open for Jet.

"Thanks," Jet said to her mother. "Can you lock up for me?"

"Of course." Marcel nodded, hiding her surprise that Jet obviously wanted her to go to the hospital as well.

On the way to the hospital, Jet sat in the back seat with Fadiyah on her lap. Marcel could hear her talking to the girl.

"It's okay baby girl, it's okay, we're almost there, just hold on to me, okay, it's okay…"

"I don't want to hurt you," Fadiyah whispered at one point.

"You won't hurt me, honey, it's okay, you squeeze as hard as you need to, okay?"

"You would not hold my hand in Iraq…" Fadiyah said softly.

"That was different," Jet said, grinning. "I would have broken your hand then."

"I do not want to hurt you now…" Fadiyah said.

"Shhh… Honey, you won't hurt me, I promise…" Jet said, kissing her forehead gently.

When Todd pulled up to emergency, Jet looked at him. "Get someone, please."

Todd nodded, responding to the authority in his daughter's voice.

He came back with a doctor a few minutes later, and opened the back passenger door where Jet sat.

"What have you got?" the doctor asked.

"Twenty-year-old female, good health, she's had a fever all afternoon, and now she's having pain in the lower right abdomen."

"Do you still have your appendix?" the doctor asked.

Fadiyah looked at Jet.

"Yeah, I'm sure she does," Jet said.

"Okay, we need to get her in," the doctor said moving to take Fadiyah out of Jet's arms. Fadiyah immediately recoiled from him.

"I got her," Jet said, shifting so she could get out of the vehicle still holding Fadiyah in her arms.

The doctor looked surprised, but nodded and led the way into the ER. He took them over to a bed and told Jet to lay Fadiyah down. Jet did, but stood next to the bed, holding Fadiyah's hand and smoothing her thumb over her forehead.

"Miss, you're going to need to—"

"Yeah, I'm not moving," Jet said. "And you need to go get a female doctor. She's Shia and can't be examined by you, doc."

"But miss…" the doctor began again.

Jet held up her badge. "Just get me a female doctor, now. She's not being left alone with anyone in this place, but me, it's as simple as that."

Finally the doctor nodded, looking quite put out but he left the room to find a female doctor. When the female doctor came in, she looked shocked by Jet's presence, but she moved to the other side of the gurney to examine Fadiyah. The entire time the doctor checked her, Jet kept brushing her thumb across Fadiyah's forehead, her face right down to Fadiyah's, talking to her.

"It's okay babe, it's okay, they're going to take care of you."

The doctor called for an ultrasound and had a nurse come in to draw blood. Jet continued to talk to Fadiyah the entire time, and Jet's parents watched every minute.

"I'm fairly sure this is an appendicitis and we need to remove it now before it ruptures," the doctor told Jet. "Who is responsible for this girl?"

"I am," Jet told the doctor.

"Does she have insurance?" she asked then.

"I'm her insurance, do what you have to do, I'll take care of the bill," Jet said sharply.

"But," the doctor began, thinking that if Jet was just a cop she certainly didn't make the kind of money the surgery would cost.

"Take care of her now," Jet said, her tone dropping an octave. "Or they'll need to do surgery on you next."

The doctor hurried away, even as Todd walked over to Jet.

"Honey we can help with the bill if—"

"I got it, Dad, don't worry," Jet said, moving to touch Fadiyah's face again.

"Honey, they're going to do surgery, it'll be okay, I promise. I'll be right here when you wake up."

"Jet?" Fadiyah said, sounding scared.

"Baby, I'm right here," Jet said, touching her face again. "I'll right here till they take you up, okay?"

She glanced at the nurse who came in to prep Fadiyah for surgery. "Can you give her a sedative? I don't want her to freak here..."

The nurse looked over at Jet and then looked at Fadiyah. She nodded. "I need to start an IV, so we'll put something in that, okay?"

"Great, thank you," Jet said, smiling warmly at the woman.

A couple of minutes later, the nurse put the IV in, and Fadiyah looked afraid. Jet bent over her. "Just look at me babe… It's okay, it'll just be a little stick and then it won't hurt, okay… Look at me babe… Look at me…"

Fadiyah's eyes flickered when the needle pierced her skin, but then Jet could see that she was growing tired almost instantly.

"I love you honey… I'll be right here, okay? Right here."

Before they moved to wheel Fadiyah out, Jet looked at the doctor. "No men in the room with her at any point in time," she told the doctor. "I mean that, I'll have someone's ass if I hear anything different."

"We understand Islamic customs, ma'am," the doctor said, nodding.

"Good, adhere to them," Jet said.

After Fadiyah was wheeled away, Jet grimaced and moved to sit in the nearest chair. Her back had been screaming at her for hours, but she didn't want Fadiyah to see that, she knew the girl would focus on her instead of taking care of herself.

"Jet, are you okay?" Marcel asked, moving to her daughter's side.

"Nothing a side of mustard wouldn't help…" Jet muttered.

"What?" Marcel asked, glancing up at Todd.

"I feel like a damned pretzel right now," Jet said, leaning forward to put her chest to her thighs to try and stretch her back.

"How about a muscle relaxant?" the male doctor from earlier asked, having seen Jet struggling.

"Nah, thanks doc. I need to be alert when she comes out of surgery, but thanks."

"Let me know if you change your mind," the doctor said, nodding to Jet's parents.

Over the course of the next hour, Marcel and Todd saw that Jet was indeed agitated and worried. She got up and paced, even if every so often she winced when she moved wrong. When the doctor finally came out to talk to them, she told them that the surgery went well and that there were no complications.

"Okay, where is she now?" Jet asked.

"She's in recovery, in a private room," the doctor said, her look pointed.

"Good," Jet said, nodding. "And there will be no male nurses in the room at any time, right?"

"Right," the doctor replied. "We do have protocols in place for Islamic sensitivities."

"Well, I know it might have been a little confusing, since she doesn't wear the hijab or abaya or anything. So…"

"It's okay, we know now and it's been noted on her chart."

"When can I see her?" Jet asked then.

"I'd like to give her some time to come out of the anesthesia…" the doctor began.

"Yeah, that's the part I'm worried about. She's never been in a hospital before, and she's going to be freaked out if I'm not there when she wakes up."

"Alright," the doctor said, nodding. "Since she's in a private room you won't bother other patients, so I'll take you back," she said, motioning to all of them.

Jet followed the doctor into the room, and Jet immediately went to Fadiyah's side. She was still unconscious. Turning around, Jet pulled a chair over to the side of the bed, and sat down. Her parents sat in chairs near the end of the bed.

It was another hour before Fadiyah came out of the anesthesia, and as Jet had expected, she became very upset and called for Jet immediately. Jet was up and out of the chair instantly, her hand on Fadiyah's cheek, her voice soothing.

"I'm here, babe, right here…"

"Jet… Jet…" Fadiyah gasped, reaching for Jet's hand.

"What is it honey? Are you hurting?"

Fadiyah nodded, her eyes staring up at Jet.

Jet reached down pushing the call button for the nurse.

"Okay, I've called the nurse, try to relax babe…" Jet said, lowering her lips to Fadiyah's cheek. "Breathe slow honey… It's okay… I'm right here… Just breathe for me babe… Nice and easy… It's okay…"

The nurse came in looking at Jet.

"She needs pain meds," Jet told the nurse, without looking at her.

"Ma'am, we can't—"

"Just get ahold of the doctor and get her out of pain," Jet snapped.

The nurse jumped, but nodded and left the room.

It took another ten minutes, but the nurse finally came in with a syringe and put it into the IV. Fadiyah relaxed immediately, as did Jet.

71

Even though she was out of pain, it was obvious that Fadiyah was restless.

"What is it honey?" Jet asked her gently. "What can I do?"

Fadiyah started to turn over on her right side.

"No, babe don't," Jet said, touching Fadiyah's shoulder to stop her.

Fadiyah reached out to take Jet's hand and pulled at her.

"I need you close…" Fadiyah whispered.

Jet smiled softly. "Okay, honey, okay."

Jet looped her foot around the leg of the chair she'd been sitting in and pulled it closer to the bed. Sitting down, she leaned her upper body in close to Fadiyah. She took Fadiyah's hand in hers, tucking it into her arm leaning on the bed, and put her other hand to Fadiyah's hair, stroking it soothingly.

Once again Marcel and Todd watched the two women, and were astounded by their daughter's tenderness. They left a few minutes later, telling Jet that they'd be back the next day.

Jet slept with her hand still in Fadiyah's, waking only when the nurses came in to check Fadiyah's blood pressure and pulse.

The next day, Fadiyah was released from the hospital, and she was told to take it easy for the next couple of weeks. Marcel said that she'd be happy to stay at the house to make sure that Fadiyah was looked after when Jet had to go back to work. As they were checking Fadiyah out, they handed Jet the bill. She looked at it then pulled out her wallet, taking out a credit card and handing it to the woman checking them out. Todd and Marcel exchanged a concerned look. Fadiyah saw their look, and looked over at Jet. The woman handed Jet's credit card back, and she put it away, then signed the paperwork.

Once done, the woman handed all of the paperwork over to Jet. Jet gave them to Fadiyah, so she could push the wheelchair Fadiyah was in. Fadiyah glanced at the numbers on the receipt that was stapled to the papers, she was sure she saw that the bill was over $100,000. She glanced up at Jet who was looking ahead of them. She decided not to say anything, but she knew that Jet had just paid a very expensive bill and without any sort of concern by the looks of it.

Later that day, Fadiyah and Jet were lying in bed resting. Fadiyah reached out to touch Jet's shoulder.

"Jet..." Fadiyah said softly.

"Hmm?" Jet murmured, glancing up at Fadiyah.

"I am concerned," Fadiyah said hesitantly.

Jet moved to sit up, looking back at Fadiyah. "About what, babe?"

Fadiyah hesitated, but was determined to ask what she wanted to know. "About the hospital bill..."

"You don't need to worry about that, babe," Jet said.

"But Jet, it was so much!" Fadiyah said, her voice concerned.

"I've got it covered, babe, okay?" Jet said.

"It is too much, Jet," Fadiyah said, shaking her head.

"Well, they can't put your appendix back in, so..." Jet said, grinning.

Fadiyah gave her a narrowed look. "You know that is not what I mean."

"Can you please just believe me when I tell you I have it covered?"

"Only if you will tell me how," Fadiyah said.

"I have a trust fund," Jet said.

"What is a trust fund?" Fadiyah asked.

"It's money that my grandfather left me when he died. It's in something called a trust, which is basically an account that I was only allowed to access after I turned eighteen."

"How much did your grandfather leave you?" Fadiyah asked, still looking concerned.

Jet put her forefinger to the bridge of her nose. "Well, he left me a million, but that was a long time ago…"

"So I just cost you ten percent of what he left you. Jet, it is too much, I cannot let you do this."

Jet gave her a look that was a cross between amusement and confusion. Then she canted her head. "It's not too much and it's too late, I've already paid it."

"You can have the charges canceled."

"And then what?" Jet asked, her tone mild.

"What do you mean?" Fadiyah asked.

"I mean, just that, then what? We have them pretend like they didn't do the surgery? What?"

Fadiyah pursed her lips in a scowl. "I do not know this, but it is my debt to pay, not yours."

Jet took a slow deep breath and blew it out slowly. Reaching over, she picked up her phone and started touching the screen. Fadiyah looked at her in confusion, not sure why she was playing with her phone in that moment.

Jet looked back at Fadiyah seeing the confusion clear on her face and grinning at it. Finally, she got to the screen she was looking for.

"I don't usually do this," Jet said. "But I think you need to understand."

She then handed the phone to Fadiyah, moving to sit next to her, so she could point to the part of the screen Fadiyah needed to see.

"What is that?" Fadiyah asked.

"That's the balance in my trust fund account," Jet told her.

Fadiyah looked again at the number, staring at it for a long moment, not sure at first what she was seeing.

"But you said he left you one million…" Fadiyah said, her voice trailing off.

"Right," Jet said.

"Then there is a mistake," Fadiyah said.

"No," Jet said, shaking her head, smiling indulgently at the girl. "There isn't."

Fadiyah looked back at Jet, her look chiding. She handed Jet the phone and pointed to the number. "Clearly there is a mistake, there is an extra zero there."

Jet laughed out loud, shaking her head. "No, honey, there's really ten million in there, it's called investing. I did a lot of it."

Fadiyah looked back at her stunned.

Jet simply smiled and put her phone back on the nightstand, moving to lie back down.

Fadiyah simply stared down at Jet for a long time, seeing that Jet considered the matter resolved. When she realized that Jet wasn't going to say any more about the topic, she finally shook her head and leaned back to relax.

It was not the last time Jet had to discuss money that week. A few days after Fadiyah came from the hospital, Todd approached her when she was sitting outside smoking. Fadiyah was upstairs in bed, resting, and Marcel had gone to the market to get ingredients for a dinner she wanted to make that night.

Jet was smoking and listening to music, sitting in her usual chair, her feet on the chair across from her.

"Jet?" Todd queried when he walked outside.

Jet glanced back at him and saw the serious look on his face. Moving her foot so he could sit down, she also picked up the remote to turn her music down. Todd sat down looking cautiously at his daughter. He was sure this wasn't going to be a good conversation. He was loathe to have it with her, but he and Marcel had agreed it was important.

"Honey, we know that you really care about Fadiyah," Todd said, putting his hand on Jet's hand that sat on the table.

Jet looked at his hand, remotely thinking that things had definitely changed over this visit. Looking back over at her father, she nodded, waiting for him to continue.

"But honey, have you thought about how much it's going to cost to keep her with you?"

"What do you mean?" Jet asked.

"Well, this recent incident cost a pretty big chunk of money…" Todd said, his voice trailing off to indicate how serious he thought it was.

"And how do you know that?" Jet asked, her tone mild.

"Well, the paperwork was on the counter, honey, we weren't trying to snoop."

Jet nodded. "Trust me, Dad, I have it covered, okay?"

"Yes, Jet, but you used a credit card, that's going to cost you a fortune in interest."

"It wasn't a credit card," Jet said.

"What?" Todd asked, looking stunned.

"It was a debit card," Jet said, her grin wry. "You really think I'm stupid enough to put a hundred kay bill on a credit card?"

Todd looked back at his daughter, his look assessing. Yes, he actually had thought Jet was using a credit card to pay the bill. He felt that his daughter's spending had always been outrageous, like buying a $180,000 car and a $60,000 motorcycle because she'd gotten a bonus check. The reason he and Marcel had insisted that she stay in the house was to try and save her some money. He never imagined that his daughter paid any attention to money and smart financial moves. With the huge doctor's bill, and the obvious sign that Jet intended to take the debt on herself, her pride being as strong as it was, he and Marcel had become concerned that Jet was in over her head with trying to take care of Fadiyah. Now he realized he might need to reevaluate a little bit.

Jet could see from the look on her father's face that he had indeed thought her that foolish. She tried to give him a little bit of credit, she knew that he had no way of knowing how good she was with money. She hadn't communicated with them for years, so he wouldn't know her habits. The purchases he knew about like the Maserati and Ducati, and the fact that she worked for LAPD which paid her about a hundred thousand a year if she was lucky, would lead him to believe that she was indeed careless.

"Dad, I've got it covered, okay?" Jet told him.

"So you're using your trust fund," Todd said. "Honey, I know that a million dollars seems like a lot, but it really won't take long to—"

"Jesus, Dad! I got this!" Jet said, losing her patience.

"Jet, your pride is admirable, but you need to understand—"

"Christ…" Jet said, picking up her phone and opening her trust fund account, before shoving the phone at him.

Todd looked at the phone for a long minute, then he raised his eyes to his daughters. "You still have the whole mill—wait, that's…" His voice trailed off as he actually focused on the number.

"Yeah," Jet said, nodding at her father.

"How?" Todd asked. It had been almost thirteen years since she'd had access to the money, but the amount she'd increased it by was incredible.

"Investing, taking some risks, a few of them huge… It paid off," Jet said, grinning as she shrugged.

"I'd say so," Todd said, handing her phone back, looking quite impressed with his daughter. "Maybe you should go into stock broking…" he said, winking at her.

Jet laughed. "Nah, it's more fun to shoot at people."

Todd chuckled, that sounded more like his hardheaded daughter.

***

"That's a sad little car…" Jet said to Shenin the next day in the parking lot as they were all leaving for the day. She was looking at the rental Shenin still had, even after almost seven months.

Shenin looked at the Chevy Spark and shrugged. "It's not like my last car, that's for sure."

"What was the last one?" Jet asked.

"A Challenger," Shenin said, sighing. "Not a Hellcat like Jericho's, but it was nice…"

"What happened to it?" Jet asked.

"Wrapped it around a tree in Maryland one night," Shenin said, her tone so mild that it took Jet a minute to catch up.

"Wait, you what?" she asked, sounding alarmed.

"It wasn't my fault," Shenin said, moving to take a cigarette out.

Jet immediately moved to light it for her, since she had her own lighter out already.

Tyler barreled through the hospital doors, heedless of anyone that was in the way. She ran straight up to the nurses station.

"Shenin Devereaux-Hancock," she said, her voice breathless. "Brought in after a car accident, where is she?"

The nurse looked up at the woman standing in front of her, with her military uniform, her bright blue eyes and extremely worried look.

"Are you a relative?"

"I'm her wife, damnit! Tell me where she is!" Tyler snapped.

The woman jumped at the order in Tyler's voice, looking at the computer again.

"She's still in surgery, you can wait over there," the nurse said.

Tyler walked away, and proceeded to pace for the next three hours, only stopping long enough to hug her parents when they arrived. It took both Carl and Becky Hancock to finally get Tyler to sit down.

"Where was she at?" Carl asked.

"On the two ten headed home…" Tyler said, her voice tremulous.

"Well, we don't know anything until we know something…" Becky said sensibly.

"I know, Mom," Tyler said, doing everything she could to hold it together.

"Do they know what happened?" Becky asked then.

"Drunk driver," Tyler said. "They said he cut her off… Jesus…" she breathed. Just imagining the accident was making her sick.

She'd gotten the call in her office. "Tyler Hancock?" a man had queried.

"Yes?" Tyler had responded.

"I'm Officer Shawn Spyvey with the Maryland State Police, I'm sorry to tell you that your wife has been involved in an accident. She's being taken to Fort Washington Hospital."

"What happened?" Tyler had asked, even as she stood up pulling out her keys, and started to walk toward the door.

"Drunk driver swerved in front of her, she hit a tree. You need to come quickly."

"Thank you," Tyler had said, hanging up.

After five hours with no word, Tyler was beside herself with worry. What could be taking so long? She told herself that at least they hadn't come to tell her that Shenin was dead, but that didn't mean it wouldn't happen. Tyler couldn't even begin to imagine her life without the feisty red-head in it. She had to be okay, she just had to be.

Finally, six hours into her vigil, the doctor came out. Tyler stood nervously as the man prepared to tell her Shenin's condition. She could tell from the look on his face that it wasn't great.

"Your wife has suffered a very serious back injury," the doctor said. "We've been working for hours to repair as much of the damage as possible. There's a lot of swelling and it's going to be hard to know for a few days how much we were able to do…"

"But she's going to be okay?" Tyler asked.

The doctor looked cautious. "Her life is not in danger at this point in time, but you need to understand, Captain, that she may not walk again."

Tyler closed her eyes, feeling the room spin, relief and grief seemed to blend into one at the moment. Shenin was alive, but if she couldn't walk again, it was going to be a major blow and Tyler had no idea how Shenin would handle that.

"When can I see her?" Tyler asked.

"In a couple of hours," the doctor said.

"Thank you, doctor," Becky said, even as Carl led Tyler over to a chair, seeing how pale his daughter had become suddenly.

Becky came to sit with them. "She's going to be okay, Tyler, it's going to be fine," she assured her daughter.

Tyler was concentrating on breathing at that point, and trying to stay conscious because her mind wanted to escape from the possibilities. Shenin was alive, that's what mattered. She was alive.

Tyler sat next to Shenin's bedside the next morning, but she hadn't regained consciousness yet. Other than a cast on her arm and a couple of cuts on her face, Shenin didn't look like she'd been in an accident, but Tyler knew that what she couldn't see was what was the most hazardous to Shenin.

Shenin stirred, grimacing a couple of times, then finally opening her eyes. Tyler was standing by that time, looking down at her.

"Hi there," Tyler said softly, her blue eyes shining.

"Hi," Shenin said, her voice a gravelly whisper.

Shenin's eyes looked around her and up at the IV that hung next to her bed.

"What happened?" she asked.

"What do you remember babe?" Tyler asked looking pained.

Shenin's eyes became unfocused in her effort to remember. "I was on my way home... Some car came up fast on the left... I remember thinking he was in an awfully big hurry... He started to pull ahead of me, and I figured good riddance..." Her voice trailed off, and then she closed her eyes. "Oh shit... He swerved in front of me... He hit my front quarter panel, I tried to evade... Oh God, Ty..."

Tyler nodded. "Okay, it's okay, you're okay."

Shenin shook her head, as she started to sense something not right.

"Babe, wait…" Tyler said, as she saw the look of terror cross Shenin's face.

"I can't… Ty, I can't move…" Shenin said. "Why can't I move?" she asked, her voice now shaking.

"Honey, calm down," Tyler said, her hand touching Shenin's cheek. "It's probably only temporary, okay? The doctors worked on you for six hours. They said there's a lot of swelling right now in your spine, so it's perfectly normal for you not to be able to move right now… As the swelling goes down you'll probably regain most of your movement…"

"Most?" Shenin repeated.

Tyler breathed a slow breath out. "Yes," she said.

"But not all," Shenin said, her look changing.

"It's hard to know right now, Shen, we just have to wait and see…" Tyler said, her look cautious.

Shenin nodded, looking devastated.

Two months later, Shenin left the hospital, and there was definite movement of her feet and legs. She was to start physical therapy a week later.

Tyler came home the afternoon after Shenin's first physical therapy appointment. They'd found a woman that would come to the house, which made it a lot easier on Shenin.

Walking into their bedroom Tyler saw Shenin lying on their bed, wearing an Air Force t-shirt and shorts. She had one arm thrown up over her eyes.

"Hey," Tyler said, moving to kiss Shenin's lips.

"Hi," Shenin said, sounding tired.

"How did physical therapy go?" Tyler asked, as she removed her holstered weapon and sat down in the chair near the bed to unlace her boots.

"You mean that exercise in sadomasochistic torture?"

Tyler chuckled. "That bad, huh?" she asked, standing and unbuttoning her jacket then hanging it up.

"I don't think she got that I'm a virgin," Shenin said.

"Or maybe she did get that you're determined to work your way back," Tyler said, moving to sit down next to her on the bed, putting her hand out to touch Shenin's arm.

Shenin put her arm down, her gold eyes looking up at Tyler. "Am I just wasting my time?"

"In terms of what, babe?" Tyler asked, her voice gentle.

"I'm never going to make it back to security force, am I?" Shenin asked, finally saying what she'd been thinking for the last two months.

Tyler drew in a deep breath and blew it out slowly. "I don't know, Shen..." she answered honestly.

Shenin nodded, accepting that answer. They were both silent for a few minutes. Tyler moved her hand to Shenin's neck and started to massage the bunched muscles she felt there.

"Mmm..." Shenin murmured. "That's nice..."

"Turn over. I'll see if I can make it feel better," Tyler told her.

84

"Only if there's a happy ending at the end of it," Shenin said, grinning as she moved to turn over. She pulled her shirt off as she did, revealing a gray exercise bra.

Tyler was surprised, they hadn't made love, or anything even remotely close since Shenin's accident. Not commenting, she rubbed the overworked muscles, feeling them ease as she worked on them. Eventually she pulled out the lotion for "stress relief," with eucalyptus and spearmint scent to try and help her wife relax.

Shenin sighed, moaned, and groaned a bit as Tyler worked on her back. There were comments of, "Oh, right there" and "Ow, ow, ow" when the pressure was too much. At one point Tyler leaned down, kissing Shenin's bare shoulder and got "Mmm…" in response. She continued to move her hands downward toward the small of Shenin's back, feeling a lot of tension there.

Shenin was thoroughly enjoying the feeling of Tyler's hands on her back, not only because she was easing very sore, very tense muscles, but because it felt good to feel that connection between them again. She held her breath as Tyler's lips touched her shoulder, moaning slightly when a shudder went through her. She'd hoped that Tyler would do more, but she'd gone back to massaging at that point. Part of her knew that if she purposely tried to seduce Tyler that Tyler would probably respond, but it was that little kernel of doubt that Tyler really wanted her, that kept her from doing so.

As Tyler's hands moved lower, touching the backs of her thighs, massaging, touching, Shenin once again held her breath. She was trembling with need, and she wasn't sure how much more she could take, hoping that her comment to Tyler hadn't been taken as only a joke. Then she felt Tyler's lips at the back of her knee and she had to bite her lip to keep from groaning. In her head she was chanting "please, please, please…" And then she felt Tyler's fingers moving up her thigh and she held her breath again. When Tyler's fingertips brushed upward, she lost all control and gasped in her orgasm. Tyler moved to kiss her back and slid her hands over Shenin's skin, making her shudder again.

Tyler lay down next to her on the bed, and Shenin raised her head, looking over at her wife. There was a very satisfied smile on Tyler's lips.

"That was…" Shenin began, shaking her head. "Wow…"

"Mmmhmm," Tyler murmured, her look heated.

Shenin reached her hand out then, touching Tyler's stomach, still covered by her khaki brown shirt. She slid her hand up, her thumb brushing an already hard nipple. Tyler moaned in response. Shenin moved to lean up over Tyler, lowering her head to kiss Tyler's lips as she slid her body over Tyler seductively. Tyler's hands moved to her hips, pulling them closer, Shenin's lips moved to Tyler's neck, as she moved her body against Tyler's. Within minutes Tyler was crying out and grasping at Shenin's hips.

They lay together afterwards, breathing heavily and grinning at each other.

"I think we need a shower," Tyler said when she'd caught her breath.

"I think you're right," Shenin said, grinning.

The shower resulted in another lovemaking session, but later they lay completely sated together.

"Are you okay, babe?" Tyler asked in the semi-darkness of the room.

She was lying on her back, with Shenin's naked body still half over hers, her left arm around Shenin's waist.

Shenin drew in a deep breath, blowing it out slowly. "I'm getting there."

"But you weren't," Tyler said.

"For a while there, no," Shenin said, knowing what Tyler was worried about.

They'd been apart years before, when Shenin's request for transfer had been denied. Tyler was in Washington D.C., while she was assigned to an Alaskan airbase. She'd known she was facing another eighteen months on the opposite side of the country from Tyler. It was then that Shenin had contemplated suicide seeing no way for them to be together. Tyler had told her months later, that had Shenin actually done what she'd been thinking, it would have ended her too. She'd meant that quite literally. Tyler had no idea what she'd do without Shenin; she was the only woman she'd ever loved with every fiber of her being. Now Tyler had been worried that Shenin was entertaining dark thoughts again, and she'd been right.

Tyler closed her eyes, grimacing. "Oh honey..." she said, feeling devastated.

Shenin moved to look up at Tyler. "It wasn't bad, not like last time..." she said.

"But if you thought it at all, Shen..." Tyler said, shaking her head.

"I can't always help it, Ty. It's like my mind just goes there."

"That's what scares me to death babe..." Tyler said.

Shenin nodded, understanding what Tyler was saying, but not sure what she could do.

"Is it maybe time to look at medication?" Tyler asked gently.

Shenin looked back at her, surprised by the question. "I don't know how the Air Force would react to that. What if they just decide I'm too big a risk and kick me out?"

"They won't do that, Shen," Tyler said.

"I'm not sure about that," Shenin said, looking concerned.

"Can we talk more about it?" Tyler asked.

Shenin nodded, putting her head back down against Tyler's shoulder.

Two months later, Shenin was back to walking and running and doing just about everything she'd done before. She did however have enough lingering weakness in her back to make it impossible for her to complete the physical challenge to continue to be part of the security force. It was a hard blow for her, and it took her some time to come back from it. Tyler worried about her constantly and once again asked her about getting on medication. Shenin had soundly refused and had come up with the solution of becoming a logistics officer shortly after that.

Chapter 4

Ashley had gotten a ride into the office from Jet one afternoon, and walked into Sebastian's office unexpectedly.

"Wow," he said, when he looked up, seeing her standing in his doorway. She was dressed in jeans, high heeled boots and a sapphire-blue blouse that was both clingy and very feminine.

Ashley knew she looked good; she'd actually shocked Jet as well. She wanted to look good today.

She smiled at Sebastian and walked into his office. "So, what are you doing tonight?" she asked, casually.

Sebastian looked back at her, grinning. "Nothing much, why? What did you have in mind?"

Ashley shrugged. "I was thinking it would be cool to just hang out at your place, maybe order some dinner, watch movies or something."

"Okay," Sebastian said, nodding. "I can definitely do that," he said, smiling.

An hour later they were in his vehicle headed to his apartment. He was having a hard time keeping his eyes off Ashley. She wore just the right amount of makeup to make her blue eyes sparkle. Her hair was loose in curling waves; it looked so soft, a man could spend hours running his hands through it. The thought occurred to him many times. Hold it together, Ranger he told himself. He'd never taken so much time in his life with a woman, but he wanted Ashley to take the lead on this relationship. She'd been through so much with Jet that he felt like she needed time to adjust and figure out what she wanted. So he waited.

At his apartment he changed into faded jeans and a t-shirt, leaving his feet bare. When he walked out of his bedroom he saw Ashley standing in the kitchen at the counter. He'd given her a small stack of take-out menus to peruse while he was changing.

Moving to stand behind her, he noted that she'd removed the heels she'd been wearing earlier, so he could easily look over her shoulder at the menu she was looking at.

"So what looks good?" he asked, his face next to hers, his hands on either side of her on the counter.

Ashely surprised him by turning around to look up at him.

"Oh, this looks pretty good to me," she said, moving to press her lips to his.

Her hands slid up his chest, one hand moving to the back of his neck to pull his face closer, her body pressing against him seductively. Sebastian moaned against her lips, and put his arms around her, his hands holding her close. As they kissed, Ashley's hands grasped at his hair, wanting so much all at the same time.

Sebastian's hands grasped her hips, and he lifted her onto the counter top, moving between her parted legs, pulling her closer as he deepened the kiss. Ashley encircled his waist with her legs, wanting him as close to her as she could get him. She felt his hands on her ass then, and it made her tremble. She pressed even closer.

"Please Sebastian, please..." she moaned against his lips.

After a few more minutes of kissing, she tore her lips away from his and moved them to his ear. "I want you inside of me..." she said, her voice a jagged whisper.

"Jesus..." Sebastian groaned, as desire shot through him instantly.

He pulled her blouse up and off over her head, setting it aside his hands making quick work of her bra as well. Her hands moved to remove his shirt, then reveled in the muscles and taut skin of his chest.

Within minutes, his body slid inside hers and she was sure she was going to explode. His groan matched hers as he felt her body so tight against him. They both cried out in their release moments later. Sebastian held her against him, feeling his heart slamming against his chest wall. He could not believe the powerful orgasm that had ripped through him, he only thanked the man-gods that she'd orgasmed at the same time he had, otherwise he'd have been giving up his man card for sure that night.

Ashely leaned against Sebastian, feeling almost dizzy with the incredible feelings flowing through her body. She had no idea what this meant, but she knew that she had needed this man desperately, and it felt good that she obviously had excited him to the point of no return as well.

Sebastian slid his hands down her body, over her legs, and pulled them up to wrap around his waist again. He then put her arms up around his neck.

"Hold on," he told her softly as he picked her up.

He carried her to his bedroom where he laid her gently on the bed, and then he lay down next to her, one leg thrown over hers, his arm around her waist, his face pressed against her neck. Ashley's hands caressed his arm that lay over her, simply enjoying the feeling of him against her. He smelled incredible, and his body was definitely everything she'd dreamed and more. The man definitely took care of himself.

Sebastian was still trying to recover from their first encounter. He hadn't been that far out of control of his own body for many years now and it had truly shocked him. Ashley's demand for him had just about sent him over the edge that second. It had just been so unexpected from her. In his head he'd made her into this wallflower, and had figured it would take a while for her to get to the point where she wanted more than the kisses they'd shared. Part of him had also wondered if she was, in fact, truly a lesbian and wouldn't therefore find sex with him satisfying. He knew that was part of his hesitation as well, and he hadn't been sure his ego could withstand that level of decimation. So the fact that she had made the first move, and had, in fact, been quite demanding in her desire for him had been a killer combination.

Levering himself up on an elbow, he looked down at her.

"So," he said, his voice rich and sexy. "That was… uh, unexpected."

"Was it?" she asked, glancing over at him, her blue eyes reflecting surprise.

Sebastian looked back at her, his look assessing. "Well… yeah," he said honestly.

Ashley moved to turn over on her side, looking at him.

"Sebastian, I've wanted you since the wedding," she told him.

Sebastian looked back at her blankly. "Really?" he asked.

"You didn't know that?" she asked.

"Uhhh, no," he said.

Ashley looked at him, her look reflecting amusement at his obvious lack of intuition.

"Hey, gimme a break, I'm not usually the runner up to a lesbian rock star," he said with a wry grin.

Ashley laughed at that. "Is that right?"

Sebastian shrugged. "I was giving you time."

Ashley nodded. "And that makes you a much better man than most."

"Well, I've learned a thing or two about respect for women. My best friend is pretty vicious when she eviscerates me for being a macho asshole."

Ashley laughed again. "Kash is that bad huh?"

"She keeps an eye on me, that's for sure," he said, smiling like he didn't mind.

"As any good best friend would," Ashley said.

"Uh-huh," he said, grinning.

Ashley reached out to touch his shoulder, tracing down his chest to a thin white scar near the center.

"What's this from?" she asked.

"Bullet," Sebastian said, his tone so casual that Ashley didn't really think about what he'd said for a minute.

"Wait, did you just say bullet?" Ashley asked.

Sebastian grinned, nodding.

"When you were a Ranger?" she asked.

"Nope," he said. "This was about four years ago now."

"Oh my God, Sebastian, what happened?" Ashley asked, surprised by his generally casual attitude.

"I was protecting a Deputy AG, and some guy took a shot at her," he said.

"You mean you," she said.

"No, I mean her. I did my job and blocked it."

"With your own body?" she asked, her look aghast.

"That's why they call it bodyguard, babe," he said, winking at her.

Ashley shook her head. "How close was it to your heart?"

"Took out a little chunk," he said, grinning.

"Seriously?" she asked, paling slightly.

He nodded.

Her finger traced the scar, her look intent. Then she looked up at him.

"Is that why you said you're bullet proof?" she asked him.

"Pretty much."

Before he, Jet and Skyler had left for Iraq to rescue Fadiyah months before, he'd promised her to take care of Jet and Skyler. He'd told her then that he was "bullet proof." At the time it had sounded like bravado, now she saw what he meant. He'd escaped death.

Inexplicably, her eyes filled with tears.

"Hey…" he said, pulling her to him, and hugging her.

"You protected someone with your life…" Ashley said, against his chest. "Who actually does that?"

"Uh," he stammered, "me, other body guards."

Ashley just lay against him and she shook her head again.

Sebastian grinned. "I guess accountants don't do that kind of thing, huh?"

Ashley laughed softly. She'd told him about her ex-husband, the accountant, who'd been so completely ungallant that Jet was manlier than he had been.

"I don't think there are too many people who would do what you did, Sebastian."

"I think you'd be surprised by how many people you know, have done just that," he told her.

She looked up at him. "Who are you talking about?" she asked.

"Well let's see, there's Kash, who's put her life in danger more than once for Sierra. Then there's Jericho who stepped into a knife to keep someone from hurting Zoey; Quinn, who protected Xandy with her life more than once. And of course there's Jet who put her life in danger by not only going back to Iraq to save Fadiyah, but also took a bullet for her…"

"I think I see your point," Ashley said, grinning.

Sebastian nodded. "Thought you might."

She looked back up at him then. "That doesn't make what you did less amazing, Sebastian."

"If you say so," he said, grinning.

"I say so," she said, leaning in to kiss him again.

95

"Mmm…" he murmured against her lips. "Keep talkin' honey," he said, deepening the kiss then.

They made love again. This time Sebastian managed to keep his self-control longer, but when she started telling him how good he felt inside her, he had to kiss her into silence lest he lose that control again. Afterwards, they lay panting together, her body over his, his hands keeping her there.

"Jesus, did Jet teach you to talk like that?" he asked her, his tone still husky.

She grinned. "She taught me to take what I want."

"Not sure if I want to kiss the girl or kick her ass…" he muttered.

Ashley laughed softly, moving to kiss his chest, her lips lingering on the scar.

They spent the rest of the night alternately talking and making love, stopping only briefly to have dinner. They were totally enthralled in each other and the time just seemed to stop.

At one point, Ashley looked at the clock and saw that it was two in the morning. She moved to get up.

"Where you goin'?" he asked tiredly.

"Just going to go text Jet to let her know where I'm at."

"You need to report to her?" he asked, sounding slightly annoyed.

"No," Ashley said, her look flickering at the tone she thought she heard. "I just don't want her to worry."

When she came back into the room, she sat down on the bed, and looked at him.

"Do you have a problem with Jet?" she asked him.

Sebastian grimaced slightly, then moved to sit up, his knees up, his arms draped over them. "I have a problem with Jet when it comes to you, yeah."

"Why?" she asked him.

He looked back at her for a long moment, trying to decide what to tell her. Blowing his breath out, he shook his head.

"I just feel like she kind of screwed you over," he said, honestly.

Ashley's brow furrowed, then she shook her head slowly. "Sebastian, she didn't screw me over at all."

Sebastian gave a short laugh, looking cynical which shocked Ashley.

"What do you think she did?" she asked him, trying to understand what he was thinking.

Sebastian pressed his lips together. "This thing with Fadiyah…" he said, his voice trailing off.

"Sebastian, I knew she was in love with Fadiyah before you ever left for Iraq," she said.

He looked back at her surprised. "You did?"

"Oh yeah," Ashley said.

"And that didn't bother you?" Sebastian asked.

"Sure it bothered me, but only because I was stupid enough to fall for Jet when I knew I shouldn't."

"She let you fall in love with her."

"Let me?" Ashley countered, raising an eyebrow, much like Jet did when she thought someone was crazy.

"Yeah," he said, his look annoyed.

"You think she could control whether or not I fell in love with her?" she asked him then.

"She could have tried," he said. "She could have stayed away from you."

Ashley grinned. "How many women have fallen in love with you, Sebastian?" she asked. "Or don't you know?"

"What's that mean?" he asked.

"Because I'm betting they all knew about you, what I know about Jet, that falling for you was a dumb thing to do, and they certainly wouldn't tell you."

Sebastian looked back at her, and he truly had no answer for that. Yes, there had been women who'd fallen for him, who he'd had to let down as gently as possible. Including the lawyer he'd protected with his life... *Son of a bitch!* ricocheted through his head.

Ashley nodded as she saw him make the connection to what she was saying.

"And you need to know that Jet was always completely honest with me, Sebastian. She never led me to believe that she and I would ever be anything but lovers and friends."

"But you wanted more," Sebastian said.

"Yeah, I did," she said, looking self-effacing. "So I basically set myself up for the hurt."

Sebastian looked back at her, not sure how to feel. He wanted to be mad at Jet for what she'd done to Ashley, but here Ashley was defending her. It bugged him.

To avoid the rest of the discussion, he reached out taking her hand and pulled her to him, kissing her and in turn making love to her again. They spent most of the weekend in bed, exploring every inch of each other's bodies and thoroughly enjoying themselves in the process.

***

It was Friday night and Jet had invited Shenin to join her and the rest of the girls at the club. Shenin had agreed, even letting Jet pick her up at the apartment she was currently sharing with her dog. Jet greeted Muffit with pets and Muffit had been very excited to meet someone new. Fadiyah had fallen instantly in love with the dog, speaking to her in Arabic.

"What's she saying to my dog?" Shenin asked Jet.

"That she's the prettiest most wonderful dog on the planet..." Jet said, smiling, happy that Fadiyah was finally feeling better.

"Well, that's true," Shenin said, smiling too.

"Where'd you get her?" Jet asked.

"Iraq," Shenin said.

Fadiyah looked up at Shenin, and Jet looked shocked, "Seriously?" she asked.

"Yeah," Shenin said, nodding, her look at the dog fondly.

Muffit was always there, it was the thing she focused on when things were at their worst and most desperate. She would lie on the floor of the cell, and put her hand through the bars and Muffit would lick her hand and nuzzle it to get her to pet her. It was the only bright spot there...

Later at the club, Jet noticed that Shenin had a few shots of Absinthe, a drink that was almost one eighty proof, and then started drinking beer. Jet exchanged a look with Skyler and they made a silent deal to keep an eye on the red head. When Shenin made her way to the dance floor alone, Jet nodded to Skyler. Skyler walked out to the floor, moving to intercept a woman who was zeroing in on the red-headed Air Force captain.

Shenin was dressed in snug fitting black jeans and an emerald-green silky tank top that showed off her curves alluringly. The black heels she wore only enhanced the fit of the jeans. Her makeup was dark enough to make her gold eyes seem to glow. She was undoubtedly a beautiful woman; Jet and Skyler knew they were going to have their hands full all night, especially with her getting obviously drunk. They also knew that they needed to protect her.

Cat, Natalia, Jovina, and Raine moved to join Shenin on the floor, doing their best to help protect the newest member of their group. They'd seen Skyler and Jet doing their best, but knew that since neither danced other than slow songs, they could only do so much. Even so, Jet and Skyler took turns standing near the women to keep an eye out. Butches on the prowl had already seen that Shenin wasn't with any of them, so thought she was fair game, even though she wore a wedding ring. Her wife wasn't in evidence.

"How does this always happen?" Jericho asked as Zoey and Xandy went to join the group. "We lose our women to other women..."

"Still a nice show..." Quinn said, grinning as she watched her girlfriend dance.

"Indeed..." Jericho said.

"You two ogling the girls?" Devin asked as she walked up with another drink in her hand.

"As any good butch would," Quinn said, grinning.

"Hey, my butch is out there protecting another woman..." Devin said.

"Yeah, that's 'cause the one that she belongs to isn't here to do it," Jericho said.

"That sucks," Devin said, sadly.

"Yeah," Quinn said. "But we gotta do our part... Aw crap..." she said, seeing a big butch moving in on Shenin and seeing both Jet and Skyler moving toward her. "Goin' in," she said, pushing off the table and walking toward the dance floor.

"And there she goes..." Jericho said, grinning. "Guess I'll just stay here and protect you two," she said, looking over at Fadiyah and winking.

"Or not..." Devin said, as things started to get out of hand.

"Or not," Jericho said, moving toward the dance floor as well.

The tall butch was not taking "no" for an answer and Jet was now holding Shenin away from her as Skyler and Quinn tried talking to her. The woman was very obviously drunk and was trying to push past Skyler and Quinn. Jericho walked up, flashed her badge at the woman and started pushing her back.

"What's going on out there?" asked someone from behind Devin.

"Oh, a friend of ours is a bit drunk and we're trying to keep her safe."

"Safe?"

"Yeah, her wife isn't here, so the girls are trying to keep the riff raff away," Devin said, glancing at the person she was talking to. "Oh… you're Tyler," she said, looking surprised.

Tyler looked at the smaller woman, shocked that she knew her. Then she located Shenin on the dance floor being held by a black-haired butch.

"Son of a bitch…" Tyler growled as she strode toward the dance floor.

"Wait!" Devin yelled. "Crap, shit, son of a bitch!" she muttered as she took off after the new comer.

"Get your hands off my wife, now!" Tyler said from behind Jet.

Jet and Shenin turned together, both stunned by the statement.

"Ty?" Shenin said, her voice reflecting her shock.

"Tyler…" Jet said, grinning, as she let go of Shenin and held up her hands. She was not interested in getting into a fight with the security force Captain she'd heard so much about.

Shenin launched herself at her wife, and Tyler grabbed her up in a hug.

"I got you, babe… I got you…" Tyler said, holding her wife against her.

"Now that's more like it…" Skyler said, walking up to stand next to Jet.

"I'd say," Jet said, grinning.

"You see that?" Jericho said to the woman she was still dealing with. "If I'm not mistaken, that's her wife, and that's a particularly lethal member of the Air Force Security Force, and I don't think you want to deal with her, do you?"

Tyler was still in uniform, and she looked every bit the soldier, even as she held her wife. The woman looked at Tyler and decided between what she'd heard and seen, maybe it was a better idea to find someone unattached.

Jericho nodded as the woman walked away, and walked over to the group, who were now watching Tyler and Shenin's reunion with fascination.

Shenin pulled back just enough to look up at Tyler, her eyes shining.

"Are you really here? Or am I so fucked up I'm hugging someone I don't even know?"

"You better not be," Tyler said, grinning, touching Shenin under the chin and guiding her lips up to hers to kiss her.

Shenin sighed against her lips, wrapping her arms around Tyler's neck and pressing against her. Tyler picked her up in her arms, Shenin wrapped her legs around her waist and everyone cheered as they continued to kiss. After the horror of Don't Ask, Don't Tell had been abolished, any reunion of a service person with the love of their life was always met with cheers from the gay community. This moment was no different.

When Tyler and Shenin finally finished kissing, Tyler let Shenin down carefully. Shenin grabbed her hand dragging her over to Skyler and Jet and the rest of the group. She introduced her to everyone. Tyler shook hands and nodded to the people in the group, her eyes continually straying back over to Skyler and Jet.

The waitress came by at one point. "Everyone wants to buy you two a drink," she said winking at them. "What are you drinking?"

"Shock Top," Shenin said. "And water for me, please, I need to sober up here a bit," she said, grinning.

She was sitting on a bar stool, with Tyler standing next to her, Tyler's eyes still scanning the room.

"At ease, captain," Shenin said, seeing that Tyler was mentally patrolling.

Tyler looked over at her, grinning. "So what was that I walked into?" she asked.

"Hell if I know," Shenin said. "I was dancing with my friends, and the next thing I know some woman's trying to grab me. I wrenched away from her, which pissed off my back, and then Jet's there grabbing me and holding me away from the woman while Skyler, Quinn and eventually Jericho go at her... It was crazy!"

Tyler nodded, then looked her wife up and down. "And it couldn't have had anything to do with how hot you look right now, right?"

Shenin looked back at Tyler, her look amused. "You think I look hot?"

"Wasn't that my point?" Tyler countered.

"No, I think your point—" Shenin began, stopped by her wife's lips on hers.

When their lips parted, Shenin smiled up at Tyler. "How long are you here for?" she asked then.

"I've got four days," Tyler said. "Do you have time to spend?" she asked.

Shenin grimaced. "Unfortunately, tomorrow completely sucks," she said. "We're wall to wall with ops, but after that..."

Tyler nodded, trying to hide her irritation and disappointment that Shenin had other things to do. She knew it wasn't fair of her to show up and expect Shenin to be completely free, but she had hoped that since part of the time was on the weekend, she'd at least get the first couple of days with her. At this point, though, she was just happy to be with her wife again.

A slow song came on then and Shenin took Tyler's hand, taking her out to the dance floor. Tyler took Shenin in her arms, holding her close and danced with her. Oddly enough, the song that played was one they'd danced to years before, and before they'd gotten together as a couple. It was "Kiss the Rain" by Billie Myers.

Tyler remembered listening to the words and thinking the lyrics were far too close to home then. Shenin was leaving to go to Officer Training School the following day. Shenin was straight and she'd discovered months before that her extremely chivalrous best friend was gay. Tyler had been the one that had come back from a date to hold her during a thunderstorm, and the one that had wanted to kill a member of the Thunderbirds for trying to force himself on Shenin.

They had danced at a party in Shenin's honor way back then, and Tyler, who had been desperately trying to ignore the fact that she was in love with her straight best friend, had been saddened by the lyrics. She'd known that everything had been about to change for her and Shenin, and that she might never see Shenin again.

She'd wanted so much to hold on to that night. In the end, Shenin had tried to get her to kiss her, because she'd wanted to know if what she'd been feeling for Tyler was something. Tyler had refused, not wanting to condemn Shenin to the life of hiding who she really was from everyone, especially the military during Don't Ask, Don't Tell. It had been a particularly rough time for both of them.

"You remember this song?" Shenin asked as they danced.

"I do," Tyler said, nodding.

"That was so bad that night…"

"Yeah," Tyler said, shaking her head. "I wanted you so much and it just felt like the whole world was coming to an end…"

"But you wouldn't kiss me."

"Because you were straight," Tyler said, smiling.

"Because you were scared," Shenin countered.

"Yeah, that too," Tyler said, nodding.

Shenin sighed, leaning into Tyler. "It's so hard sometimes, re-membering all that… When you were hurt…"

"When you were shot…"

"Oh yeah," Shenin said, nodding.

"That was the first time I realized I was in love with you, you know?"

"Was it?" Shenin asked.

"Yep, when I just about passed out at seeing you hurt, I knew I'd fallen for you."

"Oh Ty…" Shenin murmured. They'd been through so much be-fore they'd even become a couple, and it never seemed to end for them.

She lay her head against her wife's shoulder, just wanting things to be right again, and knowing it wasn't possible. She would, however, enjoy this time with her wife.

Tyler showing up in Los Angles this way reminded Shenin of the time she'd shown up in Eielson, Alaska at the air base there. Tyler had been injured in Iraq, nearly killed by an IED. Shenin had been beside herself with worry. Tyler had gone through three surgeries to repair the damage her body had sustained. They had been in contact as often as possible during that time, but one day Tyler had shown up at the base, surprising her. It had been the most incredible thing Shenin had ever had anyone do for her.

It had been the beginning of their physical relationship. Although they'd been in love with each other for much longer, the distance had kept them separated. Much like distance was doing now.

Jet and Skyler watched the two dance together.

"And all is right with the world?" Skyler asked Jet.

"Dunno," Jet said, looking perplexed. "She almost looks sadder now..."

Skyler shook her head slowly. "Something's goin' on there," she said wisely.

"Yeah..." Jet said, curling her lips in worry.

"Guess we're gonna have to figure this one out?" Skyler said then.

"Probably," Jet said.

Both Jet and Skyler understood what underlying tensions could do to people, Skyler more than anyone. It had almost cost her relationship with Devin a few times. They both really liked the sexy little red head and could easily sense that she had a lot of demons inside of her. Being the type of people they were, they wanted to help.

Tyler drove Shenin back to the apartment she was renting. She noticed that Shenin was quiet, but she didn't want to say anything, not wanting to cause any tension. Shenin opened the door to her apartment and Muffit greeted her, and then went crazy at seeing Tyler again too. Tyler sat on the floor of the entryway to give Muffit a proper petting as Shenin looked on smiling.

"She seems to like it here," Tyler said, smiling. "Of course, she's with you, so naturally she would."

Tyler moved to stand. "I need a shower," she said.

"Okay," Shenin said, taking her into the bedroom and showing her where the bathroom was.

"I'll be out in a few, okay?" Tyler said, leaning down to kiss Shenin's lips softly.

"Okay," Shenin repeated.

When Tyler emerged from the bathroom she was dressed in a tank top and shorts. She walked into the bedroom setting aside her toiletries bag and glancing at the bed. Shenin was lying on her side, completely naked, but her look was faraway. Tyler stood looking at this woman she was married to, taking in the smooth skin, the lean muscles in her legs and arms, the curve of the hip her forearm rested on and the curve of her breasts. She really was the stuff fantasies were made of and Tyler felt fortunate that she was the one person that got to see her this way.

Walking over to the bed, Tyler knelt down to get down to eye-level with Shenin's gaze. Shenin's eyes shifted to her and she smiled softly. Tyler reached out her hand touching Shenin's cheek, her blue eyes searching Shenin's.

"You with me here?" Tyler asked softly.

Shenin nodded, looking tired.

Tyler moved to stand and walked around the bed, getting in behind Shenin, and pulling her back against her chest, wrapping her arms around her. Shenin snuggled against her, sighing.

"I love you…" Tyler said, nuzzling Shenin's temple with her lips.

"I love you, Ty…" Shenin said, her tone soft.

"Are we okay, babe?" Tyler asked then, keeping her voice gentle.

Shenin turned over in her arms, looking up at her. Instead of answering she moved to kiss Tyler's lips, sliding her hands up her body, making her shudder. Shenin pushed Tyler onto her back, moving her body to cover Tyler's as she continued to kiss her. Tyler's hands held her back, holding her close as their lips met over and over.

Shenin pulled at the tank top, removed it and pushed off the shorts as well, removing all barriers between her and her wife's skin. Tyler gasped as Shenin touched her, her lips moving lower to her nipples and making her writhe. Crying out in her release, Tyler grasped at Shenin's shoulders, then pulled her up to fasten her lips to Shenin's again, moving to push Shenin back, taking the dominant position to make love to her wife.

Once they both lay sated and trying to catch their breath, Tyler pulled Shenin into her side, her arm wrapped around her, her hand at Shenin's waist, stroking her skin. Shenin's hand rested on Tyler's smooth lightly-muscled stomach, her thumb brushing back and forth gently. Her head rested in the hollow of Tyler's shoulder; they fell asleep that way.

Tyler woke the next morning early, since she was still on East Coast time. Shenin was curled up next to her, with her hand still on Tyler's stomach. Tyler put her hand over Shenin's, stroking her fingers lightly.

She saw that Muffit had joined them on the bed somewhere during the night and she lay behind Shenin's knees. Lying in the semi-darkness of the room Tyler thought about her first meeting with Muffit.

Tyler had finally gotten permission to go to Iraq with the rescue team being sent for Shenin and the others in her team. She was told that under no circumstances was she going to be on the team that went in, but that she could be there for when the team arrived back with the soldiers being rescued. It went against everything Tyler wanted, but she also knew better than to argue too much, because she knew they could make her wait back in the States for Shenin to come home and no one knew how long that could be.

As it was, they weren't completely sure that Shenin and her team were still alive. The terrorists had claimed they were, but even if they were alive, there was no way to know how they'd been treated or if they were wounded. Tyler was dying a little every day that she didn't know how Shenin was. They'd been in captivity for two weeks. Fortunately the terrorists had wanted to bargain, otherwise Tyler knew she'd have never seen Shenin again, and she didn't want to begin to think about what Shenin's death would have been like. Middle Eastern terrorists weren't known for their gentle treatment of American women, especially not soldiers.

As the team left to meet the terrorists, Tyler paced. Every instinct she had screamed at her to go after them, but she knew she'd be in direct violation of her orders, and it could get her thrown in jail. The last place she wanted to be when Shenin got back was in jail for insubordination. It was an agonizing two hours; Tyler was fairly certain she was going to go out of her mind. Then she heard the Humvees on the way back in.

She stood at the flight line, waiting. Each of the members of Shenin's team got out, they were all skinny and dirty and there looked like a few injuries. Then Shenin got out of the Humvee and Tyler ran to her.

Shenin was crying immediately as Tyler picked her up gently, cradling her and kissing her forehead, just thankful that her wife was alive.

"I got you babe... I got you..." Tyler said against Shenin's forehead.

She turned following the team leader's direction to take Shenin into the medic to get checked out. That's when there was a ruckus and suddenly there was a loud barking and Tyler could feel something tugging at her BDU legs.

Glancing down, she muttered. "What the hell?"

"Muffit, stop!" Shenin ordered.

The dog immediately let go of Tyler's pants leg and looked up at Shenin, wagging her tail.

"A dog?" Tyler asked, looking at Shenin.

"She saved me," Shenin said.

"A dog," Tyler repeated then, nodding.

She started walking again, glancing back to see that the dog was still sitting where she'd been. Tyler whistled and Muffit came on the run.

It was another hour before Shenin's alarm went off. Tyler was still lying with Shenin against her. Muffit had noticed that Tyler was awake and had moved over to Tyler's left side to be pet and snuggle with her other owner. Shenin stirred, which had Muffit crawling across Tyler to lick Shenin's face.

"Ugh! Good morning, Muffit, sheesh!" Shenin said, laughing.

She looked up at Tyler then. "How long have you been awake?" she asked, knowing her wife well enough to know she'd been awake for a while already.

"'Bout an hour," Tyler said, grinning.

"That's not too bad," Shenin said, moving to kiss Tyler's lips.

"Nah, I was tired," Tyler said.

"Uh-huh," Shenin said, biting her lip her eyes shining.

They got up a few minutes later. Shenin showered and got ready for work. Tyler pulled on jeans, black cowboy boots and an Air Force t-shirt and a security force hat, her long curly hair pulled back into a pony tail.

She was shocked when Shenin walked out of her walk-in closet wearing faded boot cut jeans, her heeled Harley Davidson boots and an army-green shirt covered in studs and rhinestones, with the words Rock Star and two crossed guitars on it that clung attractively to her curves.

"That's your work outfit?" Tyler asked, leaning against the wall, her look shocked.

Shenin looked at her through the reflection in the mirror as she brushed her hair.

"Well, I only wear my uniform when I know I'm going to the base. They are kind of an undercover outfit there at the DOJ, so they really try not to call attention to themselves. Uniforms tend to be a dead giveaway…"

"Hmmm," Tyler said, looking speculative.

Shenin looked at her in the mirror, knowing that Tyler definitely didn't like that she was wearing civilian clothes. As usual she wore makeup that matched the color of shirt she wore, and she added earrings and a dog tag style necklace with a rainbow stripe down one side. Tyler watched her every move. Shenin was used to Tyler watching her put on makeup and get ready to go places. It was one of the things she loved about Tyler; she was so fascinated with everything she did when it came to being a "girlie girl" as Tyler liked to call it. At the moment, however, Shenin was fairly sure that Tyler's tension was rising with every accessory she added, with the exception of her wedding ring that she put on last.

"Ready?" Shenin asked, refusing to comment on Tyler's tension.

She knew that she wasn't doing anything different than she ever did in getting ready for work, so if Tyler wanted to make an issue out of it, she'd need to start it. In the kitchen, Shenin poured her coffee into a cup and looked at Tyler.

"Do you want coffee?" she asked.

"I'm good," Tyler said, shaking her head.

Shenin gave Muffit treats, getting her to sit and catch pieces of the treats in the air. Tyler watched, grinning.

"She's learning quick," Shenin told her.

"She's smart, like her mom," Tyler said, winking at the dog.

They walked to the door, and Tyler picked up Shenin's gear bag, shouldering it.

Shenin smiled. It was the way her wife was, always picking up the heavy stuff for her.

At her rental car, Tyler raised an eyebrow.

"Yeah, yeah, I know," Shenin said, shaking her head as she opened the trunk so Tyler could put the gear bag inside. "Jet was just telling me how pathetic it was yesterday."

As Tyler got into the passenger seat, putting the seat back and looking around the interior, she commented, "Well, I imagine next to a Maserati, pretty much any car looks pathetic."

Shenin chuckled, as she started the car. "True."

They'd no sooner gotten on the road than Shenin's phone rang. She turned down the radio and hit the hands free.

"Devereaux," Shenin answered.

Tyler glanced over at her; it was strange to her that Shenin was using her maiden name. She knew that Shenin hyphenated her maiden and married name, but it just sounded strange to her that she answered the phone that way.

"Hey Dev, it's Cat."

"Good morning, what's up?" Shenin asked.

"Just checking on my air support this morning," Cat said, smiling at her end.

Shenin narrowed her eyes in thought. "I've got you with a C-12 King Air at eleven, meeting them at Burbank airport. Your pilot is Jaffee."

"Got it, thanks!" Cat said.

"No problem, be safe," Shenin said.

They hung up then. Shenin glanced over at Tyler and saw that she was looking over at her.

"You use Devereaux?" Tyler asked.

Shenin looked back at her for a long moment, and then shrugged. "Yeah, it's easier to say than Devereaux-Hancock when I answer the phone."

"Hancock would be easier," Tyler said.

"For you," Shenin countered, her look mild.

Tyler wasn't sure if Shenin meant because it was Tyler's given last name or that it would be easier on Tyler if Shenin would use her married name only.

Shenin's phone rang again before they could discuss the matter further.

"Devereaux," Shenin answered, looking over at Tyler pointedly.

"Good morning…" Jet said, her tone smooth, and Shenin could hear the wide grin that she knew was on the other woman's face.

"Shut it, Jet," Shenin said, grinning too. "Did you need something?" she asked then, her tone brightening.

Jet chuckled, knowing that Shenin had picked up the habit of telling her to "shut it" from Skyler. "Do I have air support this morning?" she asked then.

"I have you with a C-12 King Air, at ten in Long Beach. I don't have your pilot's name yet, but as soon as I get it, I'll text you."

"So it's not Sky?" Jet asked.

"Jet, a King Air is fixed wing, you asked for a fixed wing and Sky's not certified on fixed wing, only copters. And while I'm sure she could probably fly it, the Air Force is funny about pilot certifications and things…"

"Oh, yeah, huh?" Jet said, grinning. "Sorry, forgot I requested fixed wing and I have no idea what a King Air thing looks like."

115

"Well, it doesn't look like a helo, that's for sure," Shenin said, shaking her head and rolling her eyes.

"Hey, I'm not the pilot here, what do I know?" Jet said.

"Well, Sky flies either a Pave Hawk or a Huey, so just remember those names."

"Ma'am, yes ma'am," Jet muttered.

"Watch it," Shenin said, grinning. "Or I'll pull your air support and send you a drone."

"I'll be good," Jet said laughing. "Thanks Dev. Talk to you later."

"Okay, be safe!" Shenin said.

After Shenin hung up with Jet, Tyler looked over at her.

"So, Jet is a cop," she said.

"Yeah," Shenin said, nodding. "She's LAPD, but she's assigned to LA IMPACT right now. She was actually handpicked by Kashena."

"Kashena is…" Tyler asked.

"Oh, that's right she and Sierra weren't there last night. Kashena Windwalker-Marshal is the Special Agent Supervisor in charge of the team Jet's on. They're COID, which is Covert Operations and Informant Development."

"And getting handpicked is not how it usually happens?" Tyler asked.

"No," Shenin said. "Kashena's team needed help, so she went looking for people to pull in, and Jet's got so much experience at informant development and operational planning that Kash wanted her."

Tyler nodded, not sure how she felt about her wife being so pro-Jet.

"And Skyler's a pilot?" she asked then.

"Yeah," Shenin said, knowing that Tyler was trying to gauge whether or not she wanted to like these people. "She was a Blackhawk pilot in the Army over in Iraq."

Tyler nodded again. "And how do they use air support?" she asked then.

"Well, sometimes for counter surveillance, other times for officer safety, or both."

"Counter surveillance?" Tyler asked, knowing what it meant, but not sure how it applied in this case.

"When the undercover officers are following a suspect, doing surveillance, sometimes the suspect will do counter surveillance maneuvers, like going into a blind alley, or into a cul-de-sac to see if he'll be followed. Without air support, the officers might follow and blow their cover. With air support, the observer or the pilot can let the officers know what the suspect is doing, so they don't blow their cover."

Tyler nodded. "Makes sense."

"And in the case of a suspect that decides to run a red light or some other crazy evasive maneuver to shake any possible tails, the officers are able to follow at a safer distance and in the event the suspect does skip through a light, the officers can stop at the light, while air support keeps track of the suspect to let the ground know where he's headed."

"Therefore, keeping the officers and the general public safer," Tyler said.

"Right," Shenin said, nodding.

"Interesting…" Tyler said, having to admit that she was impressed. "And you coordinate it all?"

"Well, I make sure they have the right aircraft for the job and the personnel to fly it. We use some Air Force pilots and other PD or SO pilots as well."

Tyler nodded. "And Jet and Skyler are obviously friends?"

"Uh, yeah, they are best friends actually," she said, her look pointed. "And they were actually a couple a long time ago."

"Really?" Tyler asked, surprised by that. "You didn't tell me how good looking they both were."

"I didn't think it would matter, since they aren't the least bit interested in me that way," Shenin replied.

Tyler's look was skeptical. "You never think anyone is interested you in that way, Shen."

"Well, in this case I'm right."

"Are you?"

"Jet's involved with Fadiyah, you met her last night, and since she went all the way back to Iraq to rescue her, I'd say she's probably pretty hung up on the girl, wouldn't you?"

"She went back to Iraq to rescue her?" Tyler asked.

"Yeah, Jet was caught in an IED blast, kind of like you were. The two men with her were killed, and she would have been dead if it hadn't been for Fadiyah's family taking her in. Fadiyah nursed her back to health."

"And she managed to bring the girl back from Iraq with her?" Tyler asked thinking that it was highly improbable.

"No," Shenin said. "She eventually went back to rescue her in ISIS controlled territory."

"Holy shit..." Tyler said.

"Yeah," Shenin said. "So I seriously doubt you have anything to worry about with Jet. She's pretty much in love with Fadiyah."

Tyler's lips twitched, she didn't like feeling stupid, but she did at that point.

"And before you think it, you're wrong about Sky too," Shenin said. "She and Devin got married right before I started here. She even rescued Devin from a mudslide at one point..."

"How?" Tyler asked, sounding shell-shocked.

"She was a rescue pilot for LA Fire, and she and her crew were just going on shift when Devin called her. Her car had gotten caught in a mudslide on Highway 1. Skyler flew the helo to where Devin was, and she and her crew rescued her."

Tyler looked surprised as she shook her head. "Okay, these people are a bit much," she said, her tone awed.

"Yeah, and that's not everything, but trust me, this whole group, those people you met last night, are probably the most incredible people I've ever been around, besides you." The last was said softly, her smile proud.

"Uh-huh," Tyler said. "I've never saved your life."

"No?" Shenin said. "How about Jean's life?"Tyler looked back at her, narrowing her eyes slightly. When Tyler had been caught by the IED, she'd saved a fellow soldier's life by pushing her out of the way at the last second.

"And what about when you sent me that ticket to Washington, D.C., and got me transferred there to be with you?" Shenin said, her tone serious. "You know you saved my life then."

Tyler grimaced, she did know that. Shenin had been depressed and considering making the ultimate decision to end her life. Tyler had been sick with worry and had pulled strings to get Devin transferred to Andrews with her, and had proposed at the airport the day Shenin had arrived.

Shenin nodded, looking vindicated.

They pulled into the lot of the building, and Tyler was distracted by the line of cars in the lot.

"Holy shit..." She muttered.

Shenin chuckled. "Yeah... they definitely love their cars here."

"You ain't kidding," Tyler said.

Shenin parked and got out. Tyler got out and moved to the trunk to get Shenin's gear bag. As they walked by cars, Shenin told Tyler what belonged to who.

"So, that's the Mas," she said, pointing to the car she was parked next to. "Obviously Jet's. The white Nismo is Skyler's; the blue Z is Cat's; the motorcycle is Raine's. Oh, and Jericho obviously rode her bike in this morning too, that's the Harley I was telling you about..."

Tyler stopped, and walked around Jericho's Harley Davidson Softail Deluxe with its custom orange and black paint and literally all the trim possible.

"That's hot," Tyler said, her voice reverent.

Shenin chuckled. "Yeah, and she drives a Challenger Hellcat too."

"I like her more already," Tyler said, grinning.

"You should see Quinn's Mach, and I've heard she's got a nineteen seventy Charger too..."

Tyler sighed, shaking her head. "So many cars, so little time..."

They walked into the building then, and Shenin signed Tyler in.

Two hours later things were hectic. Shenin had the radio on for each of the missions going on. She was monitoring the progress of all three. Tyler couldn't figure out how she did it. She was constantly updating things on the computer, making phone calls or emailing. After three hours, Shenin finally stood up and stretched. She opened a desk drawer and took out her cigarettes and a lighter.

"Come on," she said to Tyler.

She led Tyler out to the patio area where most people in the units went to smoke.

As Shenin sat down on a bench, leaning against the wall, she pulled out a cigarette and lit it.

"Still doing that, huh?" Tyler said, her tone even.

"Yep," Shenin said, looking unapologetic.

Tyler nodded, not looking happy, but saying no more about the topic.

They were both quiet for a while. Shenin looked at her nails as she smoked. Tyler watched her, still trying to figure out how to get past this barrier her wife had up around her. There were times when Tyler felt Shenin was with her completely, like the night before when they'd made love, but those times were fewer and farther between lately. It was frustrating to want to be so close to someone, but to feel them almost physically pushing you away.

"So, after today, do you have a couple of days you can take off?" Tyler asked, her tone cautious.

Shenin looked over at her, considering. Tyler wondered if she was trying to think of an excuse to say no. Finally Shenin nodded. "Yeah, I can do that."

"Great!" Tyler said, smiling. "I was thinking maybe we could head up to Sacramento to see your mom and Steve, and then maybe back to San Francisco..."

Shenin smiled, remembering their last trip to San Francisco. Tyler had just gotten out of Officer Training School and was awaiting her assignment. They'd spent time in Sacramento, where Shenin was from. Tyler had met Shenin's mother Trish and her brother Steve. They'd also taken a trip to San Francisco, Tyler's first trip there. Unfortunately, on the way there Tyler had gotten her assignment, which had been when she'd gotten Andrews Air Force Base, on the exact opposite side of the country from Shenin. It had been rough news, and Tyler had actually tried to break up with Shenin while they were in San Francisco, but Shenin hadn't allowed that. Tyler wasn't sure if Shenin would still feel that way now and it bothered her endlessly.

"We could do that," Shenin said, nodding. "But let's get a direct flight, I don't want to use transport, it'll take too long."

"Or we could drive," Tyler said.

Shenin grimaced. "That's a long drive, Ty."

Tyler nodded, wondering if the real reason Shenin didn't want to drive was that they'd be stuck in a car for hours and might possibly talk about things she didn't want to talk about. It worried Tyler that Shenin was so quiet, it was never a good thing when Shenin was quiet. And she'd been quiet a lot lately.

"Okay, so we'll catch a flight and rent a car," Tyler said, nodding, pulling out her phone to look up flights.

Shenin stubbed out the first cigarette and lit another.

"Chain smoking now, huh?" Tyler said, without looking up from her phone.

"Technically it's only considered chain smoking if you light the next cigarette from the one you've just finished," Shenin said, her tone even.

Tyler glanced over at her, her look saying, *really?*

"I smoke, Ty, don't give me a bunch of shit about it, okay?" Shenin snapped, narrowing her eyes as she messed with the butt of the cigarette she'd just put out, not looking at Tyler.

Tyler pursed her lips, knowing she wouldn't have taken that kind of tone from anyone else without an equally heated response, but she didn't want to fight with Shenin. So she pushed down the response she wanted to give.

"Okay, but if we start talking about kids again, you know you'd need to quit…"

Shenin's look was sharp and then she looked away, swallowing convulsively, but she said nothing. Tyler felt it almost like a physical blow, so she didn't want to talk about having kids anymore either? Tyler stood up, walking toward the doors to the patio and going through them.

Shenin watched her go, looking sad. She knew she was pushing Tyler away, but the last thing she wanted to talk about right now was kids again. It broke her heart to watch Tyler walk away, but she knew it was not something she could handle right now. She sat smoking the rest of her cigarette, wondering remotely if Tyler would just leave now. Her heart kicked up at the thought, but her head said, *Maybe that's what needs to happen. Maybe you just need to stop torturing her and let her go...* Shenin squeezed her eyes shut, trying to clamp down on the gut-wrenching feeling she had in reaction to that thought.

Tyler walked out the front door to the offices and continued walking, her boot heels striking the sidewalk as she strode down the street. She knew she needed to walk off the anger she was feeling. Part of her wanted to shake Shenin and make her tell her what was going on. It was maddening! She knew something was wrong, she knew something was happening to them, but she didn't know what and she had no idea how to stop it.

After about an hour Tyler calmed down enough to go back to the offices. She walked into the office Shenin was using and sat down without comment. Shenin glanced at her, but said nothing.

"I got us a flight out of LAX in the morning at nine. We'll be in Sacramento by ten," Tyler said after an hour.

"Okay," Shenin said, nodding, still looking at her computer.

Two hours later they left the office. A song came on Shenin's iPod in the car that Tyler had heard before. She turned it up, pointedly looking at her wife. The song was by Adele, and it was called "Water under the Bridge." The words talked about how it was impossible that she wasn't the one for her, and if that was possible then why had they been through so much together.

At that point in the song, Tyler reached over and touched the scar on Shenin's arm from where she'd been shot while in Iraq. The song continued and the chorus was pointed. The chorus song basically asked that if she was going to leave her, to do it softly, that their love wasn't just something in the past.

As the song ended, Tyler turned the radio back down, looking over at Shenin. She could see that Shenin had listened to the words carefully. Shenin glanced over at her seeing Tyler looking at her.

"Let you down gently?" Shenin asked, her tone affected.

"Let me down, let me go... Whatever you're planning..." Tyler said, slightly choked.

"Ty, I'm not planning anything," Shenin said, her voice quavering.

Ty looked back at her, skepticism evident on her face.

Shenin swallowed convulsively, even as that little voice told her, *She's giving you an opening... take it...* She shook her head, as much to tell the voice *No!* as it was to try and make sense of all her thoughts.

"I just can't get a handle on things right now, Ty..." she said, her voice trembling.

"Then let me help babe..." Tyler said, reaching over to take Shenin's hand. She was surprised at how cold it was.

Shenin shook her head. "There's nothing you can help with, Ty. I just need to get things squared away in my head..."

Tyler nodded, doing her best not to be hurt by Shenin's refusal to let her in.

"You scare me when you get so quiet..." Tyler told her.

"I know, I'm sorry," Shenin said. "I'm really doing the best I can at this point."

Tyler nodded, still feeling her stomach clenching.

"There's just so much distance between us babe..." Tyler said.

"Well, there is, Ty," Shenin said. "About thirty-six hundred miles."

"Babe, I'm right here and there's distance between us," Tyler said, squeezing Shenin's hand gently.

Shenin nodded sadly, knowing that Tyler was right, but not sure how to fix it.

Chapter 5

"So genius, huh?" Ashley asked Jet, glancing over at her friend as she drove.

"Jesus," Jet said, shifting gears and rolling her eyes at the same time. "Fadiyah told you that?"

Ashley laughed. "I think she's very proud," she said, smiling.

Jet gave her a foul look. "Shut up." Ashley chuckled.

"Let's talk about your weekend..." Jet said, her voice trailing off suggestively.

"What about it?" Ashley asked, her smile wide.

Jet caught the smile and laughed. "He's that good, huh?"

"And then some," Ashley said, nodding.

Jet nodded too. "Well, good, I'd say you could use that."

"What's that supposed to mean?" Ashley asked as she swatted Jet on the arm.

Jet only laughed, shaking her head.

After a few minutes of silence, Jet looked over at Ashley. "You're being careful, right?"

Ashley looked over at Jet stunned. "Are you asking if we're using condoms? Or if I'm taking birth control?"

Jet made an impatient sound in the back of her throat. "No, you idiot. I'm asking if you're guarding your heart."

"Why?" Ashley asked, surprised by the question.

Jet looked over at her, her expression telling Ashley that she was hoping she wasn't serious with that question.

"Why do you think I should guard my heart?" Ashley asked.

"Because Baz is me in male form," Jet said simply.

Ashley looked back at Jet, knowing that what she'd just said was very true, but not sure how to respond. Finally she nodded.

"I know that," Ashley told Jet.

"Do you?" Jet asked, unsure.

"Yeah, I do," Ashley said. "But I can't help that."

"You can help that by not falling in love with him," Jet said.

"Really?" Ashley said sharply. "Like I did not falling in love with you?"

Jet winced at her words. "Once bitten… Right?"

Ashley caught the look on Jet's face and wanted to let her feel it for a minute, but knowing it wasn't fair to her.

"You didn't do it on purpose, Jet, I know that," Ashley said. "Hell, I don't think you even realized you were in love with Fadiyah before you got her back here."

"But you did," Jet said.

"Yeah, I did," Ashley said, sighing.

"So, why can't you be so pre-cognitive with him?" Jet asked.

"I can," Ashley said. "And I am, trust me."

Jet drew in a deep breath and blew it out slowly. "I hope so…"

"I am," Ashley assured her.

"'Cause if he hurts you, I'm gonna have to do something about that, you know that right?" Jet said then.

Ashley looked over at Jet, expecting to see a grin, but she was shocked to see that the look on Jet's face was serious.

"No, you would not," Ashley said, her tone shocked.

Jet shrugged, looking unaffected by Ashley's denial.

"Jet, what the hell do you think you'd do? He's an ex-Army Ranger for God's sake!"

Jet nodded. "Yeah, I'd probably get my ass kicked, but…" She let her voice trail off as she shrugged again shaking her head.

"Why?" Ashley asked, still not understanding Jet's logic at all.

"Because he knows your history with me," she said, her face serious. "And he knows that he's in a position to really hurt you, and that should make him think twice. I'd make him think again."

Ashley looked back at Jet, unable to believe what she was hearing. The idea of Jet and Sebastian in a physical altercation was beyond insane.

"Why would you do that?" Ashley said, still trying to understand.

Jet looked over at her, her look going from glowering to roguish. "'Cause I love ya, kid," she said, smiling.

Ashley smiled back at Jet, tears inexplicably in her eyes suddenly.

"Quit that," Jet said, reaching her hand over to squeeze Ashley's hand.

Ashley nodded, swallowing convulsively to try and force her emotions back down. Her relationship with Jet was still a bit of a tangled mess. She loved the woman, but she knew that Jet's heart wasn't available. She adored Fadiyah and had been part of the reason Fadiyah and Jet had finally gotten together. It was bittersweet to see them together, since it was obviously love and how could she get in the way of that?

She knew her relationship with Sebastian was likely doomed, because Jet was right, he was just like her, not really into commitment. The way Ashley saw it, they had really great sex, and it was a perfect distraction from Jet and the hurt there.

She was thinking along those lines a couple of days later when she walked into Sebastian's apartment. He'd given her a key, telling her that if she just needed to get out of Jet's house for a bit, she could come there.

"Sebastian?" she called at the front door.

"Back here," he called.

Ashley walked into his bedroom; of course he had music on. She looked over and saw him lying on the bed, one arm thrown up above his head casually, wearing sweatpants and nothing else. He was definitely an incredible specimen of a man.

"You look tired," she said, as she walked over to the bed, seeing the cut on his cheek. "Ow," she said, sitting down and gently touching his face. "What happened?"

Sebastian grinned. "Suspect decided he wanted to try for the heavyweight title," he said, his tone wry.

"I take it he looks worse?" Ashley asked, chuckling.

Sebastian narrowed his eyes at her comically. "Of course he does."

Ashley laughed softly, nodding. "Still the champion, huh?"

"Yep," he said, lowering his arm, to touch her waist.

She leaned down, kissing his lips softly. He reached up with his other arm, putting his hand to the back of her head to hold her there, to kiss her again. In one smooth motion, he moved to sit up, and pulled her into him, deepening the kiss, his hand at her waist, moving to her back to pull her closer still.

Within moments, Ashley was breathless, her hands grasping at his shoulders, her nails biting into his skin. Pushing up the skirt she wore, she moved to straddle his lap, pressing against him, and making him gasp against her lips. Moving her hands over his chest, she moved her lips to kiss his neck, feeling him grasping at her back as she did. Her hands moved downward, pushing at the waistband of his sweatpants. His hands met hers, and moments later he was inside her. It was an erotic feeling that both of them still had clothes on, and it was what spurred Ashley to greater heights. She came, screaming his name and holding onto him desperately. He gave a shout a moment later, unable to hold on any longer.

Afterwards he held her against him, both of them panting.

"Jesus woman…" he breathed.

Ashley lifted her head, looking at him with a smug smile. "What?"

"Don't *what* me, you know damned good and well what…"

Ashley chuckled, reveling in the power she felt at that moment. She knew she had pushed him to his limit and felt absolutely fantastic that she'd been able to do just that.

"Liking that, huh?" he said, his tone knowing.

"I gotta say, yeah, I am," Ashley said, nodding, her eyes sparkling.

Sebastian looked at her for a long moment, his look considering. His hands slid over her blouse then, unbuttoning it and laying the sides open, his eyes on hers the entire time. Sliding his hands around her bare torso, she felt him unclip her bra, his eyes still on hers. She felt her breathing become uneven as his hands nudged the material of the bra out of the way, his thumbs brushing upward across already hard nipples. She moaned, lowering her head to his neck and biting his skin.

He removed the rest of her clothing and made love to her again. They spent the better part of the evening in that fashion.

Two weeks later Ashley walked into his bedroom again. This time he was wearing shorts and a tank top, but was in much the same position. When she heard her come in, he lifted his arm off his eyes.

He glanced at the clock. "How friggin' long did it take you to get here?" he asked.

"Like forever and a day!" she said. "Traffic in this town sucks!"

"Well, Jet's is pretty far from here," he said.

She nodded, walking over to the side of the bed.

"Are you ever going to look less tired?" she asked him, having noticed a pattern over the last two weeks that she'd been coming to see him.

"I'm beginning to wonder myself."

Ashley kicked off her shoes and climbed onto the bed, laying herself next to him and then leaning up over him to kiss his lips. He put his arm around her kissing her back.

Things got heated right away, but Ashley muttered, "Mmm Mmm" against his lips, shaking her head.

"What?" he asked, grinning.

"Have you eaten anything for dinner yet?" she asked him pointedly.

He grinned.

"And that's a big fat no," she said, shaking her head as he reached for her again. "Oh no, mister, food first. 'Cause if I know you, you didn't eat lunch either, did you?"

"Well, sure," he said, grinning.

"Liar!" Ashley said, laughing as she did, trying to avoid his hands.

"We can eat later, c'mere…" he said, pulling her to him again. Ashley kissed him, but then pulled her head back.

"Sebastian Bach, stop it!" she said, doing her best to scowl at him.

"What?" he asked, his voice amused.

"You need to eat," she told him, her voice stern, even if her eyes were dancing with humor.

He made an impatient sound in the back of his throat.

"Don't give me that…" she said, moving to get off the bed.

She went into his kitchen and picked up a few menus of places she knew delivered fairly quickly. Walking back into the bedroom she moved to sit next to where he was lying on the bed.

"Okay, your options are…" she began, even as his hand slid over her thigh.

"Can this be an option?" he asked, sliding his hand up her leg.

"Stop it!" she said, laughing. "No! You need actual food. Now, Chinese or pizza?"

"I don't care," he said, moving to nuzzle her side.

"You are not getting laid until you eat something, Mr. Bach," she said.

"That's harsh," he said, moving to sit up.

"That me, Ms. Harsh," she said, making a face at him.

"Fine, Chinese," he said sighing.

"Okay, what do you want?" she asked.

"I'll show you…" he said, grinning.

"From the menu, if you please," she said, her tone prim.

Again he made an impatient sound and said. "Fine, something… something beef."

Ashley laughed, shaking her head. She picked up her phone and made the call.

Hanging up a few minutes later she said. "They'll be here in ten minutes."

"What are we going to do with all this time?" he asked, moving to kiss her neck.

"Mmm…" she murmured. "It's not that long…" she said, her voice husky suddenly.

"It's forever," he said, sliding his hand around her. He pulled her back against his chest, reaching up to move her hair so he could have better access to her neck.

Her hands grasped his arm that was around her as she moaned softly. His arm tightened at her waist, his mouth closing on her neck, sucking as his thumb brushed upward over her nipple. She gasped, dropping her head back against his shoulder. He moved his thumb rhythmically over her nipple as his other hand slid down into her shorts. Within moments she was coming and writhing against him.

"Maybe ten minutes isn't so long after all," he said, grinning.

"Oh my God, you are so evil," she said, her voice still heated.

He stuck his tongue between his teeth playfully, waggling his eyebrows. The doorbell rang. Ashley moved to get up, and Sebastian reached for his wallet on the nightstand.

"I've got it," Ashley said. His hand grabbed hers, pulling her back down on the bed.

"I don't think so," he said, opening his wallet and handing her his credit card.

"I said I'll pay for it," Ashley said.

"And I said, that's not gonna happen."

"Sebastian…"

"Ashley…"

"They're going to leave…"

"Then I guess I get what I really want for dinner," he said, sliding his tongue over her neck. She shivered in response.

"Okay, okay," she said, moving to stand up.

Sebastian grinned. Ashley came back with boxes, forks and beers, handing him one of each. They sat on the bed, eating in companionable silence. Once they finished eating, Ashley got up and took the left overs, the empty bottles and dirty forks into the kitchen. Sebastian lay on the bed thinking that this felt good.

Ashley walked back into the bedroom again then.

"Done being all domestic?" he asked her with a grin.

"For now," she said, "but we should definitely talk about what's in that fridge of yours..."

Sebastian chuckled, holding his hand out to her. She took his hand and he pulled her down next to him, he immediately kissed her and started to remove her clothing piece by piece. She did the same to him. He made love to her then and she found that no matter what, he could always excite her beyond all reason. Once again they lay together, trying to catch their breath. Sebastian's hand stroked her skin, as he looked up at her.

"So, how's it going with moving out of Jet's?" he asked, trying not to sound too interested. He knew his attitude about Jet bugged her.

"LA is outrageously expensive," Ashley said, making a face.

"I know, trust me," he said, grinning.

"I'm not really making as much doing the freelance stuff," she said, shrugging. "So it's really not good for me to try to make a commitment to paying rent for an apartment when there might be months I don't sell a story. I'm really not sure what I'm gonna do."

Sebastian nodded, his look thoughtful.

"Well you're here a lot," he said.

Ashley grinned. "Yeah, but since Jet doesn't charge me rent, it's not like I can get credit for it, ya know?"

"Well, no," Sebastian said, his look flickering. "I meant you could just move in here."

Ashley looked back at him for a long minute, blinking a couple of times in surprise.

"There are two bedrooms, if you wanted your own…" Sebastian said, already starting to feel stupid for the suggestion.

"You don't seem like the roommate type," Ashley said. "And I know I couldn't afford half of whatever the rent is here… I mean, this apartment is so nice and all…" Her voice trailed off as she bit her lip.

"Yeah, you're probably right," Sebastian said, even as his phone started to ring. "Excuse me, I need to take this." He got up and picked up his phone, he picked up his shorts and walked out of the room.

Ashley lay on the bed, trying to figure out what had just happened. She'd been shocked by the offer of her moving in there and at first she'd been excited by the invitation, but then she'd started thinking about what Jet had said. So, just another place to stay with "no permanent house guests" stamped on her forehead. When Sebastian didn't come back she started feeling stupid, so she got up and put her clothes back on.

Finally, she went looking for him. He was sitting out on his balcony smoking and talking on the phone. Ashely stood trying to decide what to do, and finally she decided to leave. She tapped on the sliding glass door, and Sebastian glanced over at her. She waved, he nodded. She left then, still feeling incredibly stupid and awkward suddenly.

She didn't hear the yell or the impact to the wall on the balcony above her as she drove away. She drove straight back to Jet's house and went into her room, not bothering to close the door. Lying down on her bed, she gave into the good cry she needed.

Jet walked by an hour later and heard her sniffling.

"What's up?" Jet asked, standing in the doorway to her room.

Ashley looked over at Jet, tears still on her cheeks.

Jet's eyes narrowed. "Son of a bitch!" she growled and turned and walked away.

Ashley stared at the spot Jet had just stood in and then suddenly realized what Jet had thought.

"Jet! Wait!" Ashley yelled, jumping off the bed and running after Jet. But she was too late and Jet sped off on the Ducati.

Fadiyah came to the garage door, looking out as Jet took off.

She looked at Ashley. "What has happened?"

"I was just a major dumbass, that's all," Ashley said, grimacing.

Jet walked into Sebastian's apartment building, texting Kashena as she did: "You'd better get your partner in line, because he is about to piss off the wrong butch!"

Pocketing her phone, Jet pounded on Sebastian's door, her temper simmering. When Sebastian opened the door, it took everything she had not to sucker punch him, but that wasn't her style.

"What the fuck did you do to Ashley?" she asked, shoving past him to get into the apartment.

Sebastian gave a sarcastic laugh. "That's rich," he said, shaking his head and taking a drink of the beer in his hand.

Jet caught sight of the blood on his hand.

"What the fuck did you do to yourself?" she asked, immediately worried for him.

"Jesus fucking Christ, Jet. Make up your fucking mind already!" Sebastian snapped.

"What?" Jet said, shocked.

Sebastian shook his head and walked back to his balcony sitting back down. Jet could tell he'd been drinking a lot. And he looked absolutely morose. She started wondering if she'd missed something.

"What's going on Baz?" she asked him, moving to stand in front of him.

"Nothing's going on Jet Fire, you win," he said, sounding defeated.

"What exactly was I playing for?"

"Ashley, what else? Or do you need them all?" he asked, his tone sharp.

Jet looked back at him, her look perplexed. "What the fuck are you talking about?"

Sebastian just sent her a dirty look, lighting another cigarette and opening another beer.

"I think you've probably had enough to drink…" Jet said, moving to take the bottle out of his hand.

He moved to yank it out of the way and his elbow connected with Jet's cheek. She yanked her head back, but it still hit. She saw stars for a minute, but shook them off.

"Okay, keep it," she said.

"Jet…" he started. She held her hand up to stop whatever he was going to say.

"Drink yourself fucking silly, have a good time," she said and strode to the door.

Walking out into the hallway, she leaned against the wall, breathing slowly. She knew he hadn't meant to strike her but it didn't lessen the shock she was feeling.

Pulling out her phone, she texted Kashena again: "He's in bad shape, he needs you."

Shoving her phone back into her pocket, she walked out of the apartment building. Jamming on her helmet, she got on the Ducati and gunned it, roaring away from the curb in a burst of speed. She knew she was taking risks on the freeway, but the anger coursing through her kept pushing her faster and faster. Bending low over the tank of the bike, she gunned it again. She slowed the bike at the garage door, waiting for it to open. By the time she pulled the bike into the garage, both Ashley and Fadiyah were standing there waiting for her.

This is gonna go well, she thought to herself as she backed the bike into place and turned it off. She took off her helmet, keeping her head turned so they couldn't see what she was sure a fairly nasty bruise by now, if the ache was any indication. She took off her riding gloves and stuffed them in the helmet, finally climbing off the bike. She turned around and strode into the house, heading straight for the refrigerator and a beer. Reaching up above the fridge, she pulled out a bottle of Casa Noble and took that and the beer to the backyard. Fadiyah and Ashley caught up to her there.

"What the hell happened?" Ashley snapped.

Jet threw her a look. "You fucking think he looks worse?" she asked, her tone sharp.

"He did that?" Ashley asked, paling slightly.

"It was an accident," Jet said, her tone even.

"Sebastian did this?" Fadiyah asked, moving to touch Jet's cheek gently. Jet yanked her head away.

"It was an accident," she repeated, her light green eyes flashing in anger.

Fadiyah glanced at Ashley who just shook her head, shrugging.

Jet's phone chimed. She pulled it out, checked it and tossed it on the table in front of her.

"Kash is there now."

Kashena walked out onto Sebastian's balcony, seeing the state he was in. She sat down on one of the chairs.

"So, what's going on here?" she asked, her tone light.

Sebastian cast a bleary look in her direction. "Second string?"

"Oh honey, I'm always first string. I just live farther away," Kashena said, her tone as serious as the look on her face.

Her eyes dropped to the hand that was gripping the bottle of beer.

"Nice work there..." she said. "How many bones do you think you broke this time?"

Sebastian didn't answer, he just lifted the beer to his lips and drained it then set the bottle on the table.

"This about Ashley?" Kashena asked, sitting back and crossing a booted foot over her other leg.

"It isn't about anything," Sebastian said.

"Right..." Kashena said, nodding. "'Cause I don't know you or anything, right?"

"Back off Kash..." Sebastian growled.

"You don't fucking scare me, Ranger," Kashena said, her deep blue eyes narrowed slightly.

Sebastian got to his feet, taking a step toward the chair Kashena sat in, looming over her. Kashena dropped her foot to the ground, her feet set wide apart, her chin coming up slightly, her look at him direct and challenging. Sebastian narrowed his eyes seeing her challenge.

"You feeling the need to throw down big boy?" she asked him, her tone serious.

Sebastian looked back at her; suddenly he could see the tension in her neck, and the rigidity of her back. *What the fuck am I doing?* he thought suddenly. This was his best friend.

"Jesus..." he breathed, sinking to his knees.

Kashena was there instantly, holding him, her arms wrapped around him, her hand stroking his head.

"Okay, partner, okay..." she said, her tone soothing. "We got this, Baz, we got it."

He shook his head miserably. Kashena was stunned to see tears in his eyes. She helped him to his feet, sitting him in the closest chair, and pulled another chair over for herself. Sitting down, she looked him in the face.

"Tell me what happened, Baz."

"I was stupid," he said simply.

"How?" Kashena asked.

"I thought I could do better..." he said, his look still wavering.

"Better than what?" Kashena asked, still trying to figure out what was going on.

"Than Jet," he said.

"With Ashley?" Kashena asked then.

Sebastian nodded, his lips curling in disgust.

"Okay, what did you do?"

"Asked her to move in here, with me," he said, his tone self-effacing.

Kashena's mouth dropped open in shock. "I'm sorry," she said, blinking a couple of times. "Did you just say that you asked her to move in here with you?"

Sebastian nodded, looking disgusted with himself.

"Wow," was all Kashena could think of to say for a few moments. "What did she say?"

Sebastian curled his lips in a sarcastic grin. "Blah, blah, blah, I want to keep living with Jet."

Kashena couldn't help but grin at the way Sebastian said it, her look a combination of sympathy and downright amusement.

"Is that actually how she said it, Baz?" Kashena asked, trying to keep the laughter out of her voice.

Sebastian saw it, and couldn't help but start to grin too. "It was something like that…" he said, his tone still dark.

Kashena nodded her head, doing her best to look serious.

"Fuck you, Marine," he said, starting to grin.

"You may have just shocked the shit out of the girl, Baz, is that possible?" she asked him.

He shook his head, looking serious again.

"She's really hung up on Jet, Kash. I was stupid to think that I could mess with that."

Kashena's lips twitched, she didn't like seeing Sebastian so completely devastated. It wasn't him, and she didn't like it one bit.

Sebastian got up to walk into the apartment, heading to the fridge for another beer.

"You want a beer?" he called to her.

"Sure," she said, pulling at her phone and tapping out a message to Jet.

She had the phone back in her pocket by the time he walked back out.

Jet's phone chimed. Setting down the bottle of tequila, she picked it up and looked at the message from Kash. She looked over at Ashley, who was sitting in the chair next to her. Fadiyah was sitting on the other side of her, holding a cloth with ice, which Jet had thus far refused to allow her to use on her face.

"Did Baz ask you to move in with him?" Jet asked Ashley.

Ashley looked over at her surprised, then glanced at Jet's phone. "Kash?" she asked.

Jet nodded. "She's there with him now. Answer the question, Ash."

Ashley blew her breath out in exasperation. "Yeah, he asked me to move in, so what? I mean, how many women does he use that one on?"

Jet's completely shocked look should have been her first clue, but Jet's response of, "Oh, about ZERO," certainly made up for it.

"What?" Ashley asked, hoping she'd just heard Jet wrong.

"None, zip, zero, zilch, he's never asked a woman to live with him… ever, Ash."

Ashley closed her eyes slowly, feeling all the blood drain out of her head. "Oh my God... I just fucked up," she said, opening one eye to look at Jet. "I fucked up, didn't I?"

Jet gave her a tight smile and nodded.

"Oh my God..." Ashley said again, putting her face in her hands and leaning down over her knees. "I think I'm gonna be sick..."

Jet glanced at Fadiyah, a grin starting on her lips. Fadiyah looked back at her perplexed. Jet winked at her, wincing when it stretched the bruise on her cheek. Fadiyah held up the rag with the ice. Jet shook her head, laughing softly.

"Ash?" Jet said then.

"Ashley has left," Ashley said, her face still in her hands. "Ashley was incredibly stupid, and has decided to just take a leave of absence. Please leave a message."

Jet chuckled. "Ash, you need to get your ass over there and make this right."

Ashley's head snapped up, her look aghast. "I can't go over there!"

"Yes you can, and you will," Jet said, her tone sure.

"No..." Ashley said. "I can't face him again, I can't, no way."

"Do you want to live with him?" Jet asked her. "And don't bother trying to lie to me."

Ashley took a deep breath, expelling it slowly, and nodding.

"Then get your cute little ass up out of that chair, and get the fuck over there!"

"What if he won't talk to me?" Ashley asked.

Jet looked back at her. "Then take what you want."

Kashena had just left and Sebastian was still sitting on his balcony. The crowd of bottles on his table was growing, as were the butts in the ashtray. He wondered remotely if you could give yourself cirrhosis of the liver and cancer all in one day.

"Sebastian…" Ashley said from the doorway to the balcony.

Sebastian didn't turn around, merely blinking slowly, thinking that he had to be imagining Ashley's voice.

"Sebastian?" Ashley queried again, taking a couple steps out onto the balcony.

She moved closer as he lifted the beer in his hand to his lips, that's when she saw the blood.

"Sebastian!" she exclaimed, kneeling next to the chair he sat in, taking the beer out of his hand and then taking his hand gently in both of hers. "What did you do?" she asked him, turning her head to look at him.

She saw that he was looking at her with an odd curiosity in his stormy eyes.

"Oh my God, how much have you had to drink?" she asked, her eyes looking over at the series of bottles. "Oh Sebastian…" she breathed. "Come on…" she said, moving to stand and doing her best to pull him up by pulling on his wrist.

His face became amused as he moved to stand. Ashley pulled him into the house, making him sit down on the couch. She went into the kitchen then, pulling out a bottle of water from the fridge and then grabbed a dishtowel and wet it. Walking back into the living room, she opened the bottle and handed it to him.

"Drink that," she told him. When he simply looked back at her, she narrowed her eyes at him. "Drink it Sebastian." She continued to stare him down until he lifted the bottle to his lips and took a long swig.

In the meantime she knelt in front of him again, taking his injured hand in hers and gently pressing the dishtowel to the bloody spots. He jumped slightly, so she eased up on the pressure. After a few dabs she was able to see where his hand was cut, it was black and blue, and she was pretty sure he'd broken some bones.

"What were you trying to do to yourself?" she asked him, her look scolding.

Sebastian looked back at her, a smile hovering at his lips.

"You better be drinking that water," she told him, narrowing her eyes at him.

He lifted the bottle to his lips again and drained the contents. Setting it aside, he reached out and touched her cheek gently. She looked at him, her blue eyes shining.

"I'm sorry, Sebastian," she said to him, shaking her head, "I didn't mean to hurt you…"

Sebastian drew in a deep breath, blowing it out slowly as he nodded. "You did," he said simply.

"I'm sorry," she said again, moving to sit on the couch next to him. Reaching up she smoothed his hair back, her eyes looking up into his. "Please forgive me. Will you?"

"That depends," he said.

"On what?"

"On where you want to live," he said simply.

She smiled softly. "I want to live here with you."

"Then you're forgiven," he said, leaning over to kiss her lips softly.

Chapter 6

Jet knocked on Shenin's door, sticking her head in. "What are you doin' for lunch?" she asked.

"Uh," Shenin stammered, then looked back at Jet again. "What the hell happened to your face?" she asked, shocked.

Jet grinned. "Long story," she said. "Lunch?"

Shenin glanced at the clock, surprised it was already that late. "I have no plans,"

"Have lunch with me, then," Jet said, canting her head toward the front of the building.

"Okay," Shenin said, saving her work on her computer and standing up to stretch.

Jet waited for her, and then gestured for her to precede her out of the building. They walked to Jet's car and Jet opened the passenger door for her. Shenin grinned, she was just like Tyler in that respect, always the gentleman.

"What?" Jet asked, seeing the grin.

"Nothing," Shenin said, shaking her head.

On the day Tyler was leaving California, Jet walked out to her car, surprised to see someone leaning on the vehicle next to it, even more surprised when she realized it was Tyler Hancock.

"Didn't you go home today?" Jet asked as she opened her trunk and dropped her gear bag in, glancing around.

"My transport was delayed," Tyler said. "I need to talk to you, can we get out of here before Shenin comes out and sees me?"

"Okay..." Jet said, thinking this was odd.

Once in the car, Jet started the vehicle and backed out of the space.

"So what's up?" she asked, as she pulled out of the lot, glancing over at Tyler.

"I need your help," Tyler said.

Jet nodded. "Okay, what do you need?"

Tyler looked at the other woman, her look considering.

"How well do you know my wife?" Tyler asked.

Jet raised a black eyebrow. "Not near as well as I think you think I do."

Tyler shook her head. "No, I'm sorry, that's not... I was wrong about that, I know that now. I'm sorry."

"Okay," Jet said, nodding. "Then what did you mean?"

"Has she told you anything about her depression?" Tyler asked.

Jet looked surprised, then shook her head slowly. "No."

"Well, she'll probably kill me for telling you if she finds out, but she suffers from depression and sometimes it's really bad..."

"How bad?" Jet asked.

"Bad," Tyler said.

Jet grimaced, then blew her breath out. "So what do you need me to do?"

"I need you to keep an eye on her for me," Tyler said.

"What should I watch for?" Jet asked.

"She gets really quiet, withdrawn… She starts sleeping a lot."

Jet nodded, her look worried.

"Are you working on getting here to be with her?" Jet asked. "Because she needs you Tyler."

"I'm trying, but my CO keeps blocking my transfer," Tyler said, her lips curling in irritation.

"So what happens if that keeps up?" Jet asked.

"Well, my re-up date is coming up in a few months, I'll just quit."

"You'd give up the force for her?" Jet asked.

"I'd give up my life for her," Tyler said without hesitation.

Jet smiled. "Good answer."

"It's the truth," Tyler said.

"Better answer."

Jet drove to a local place and asked for a table outside. After they'd ordered lunch, Jet looked over at Shenin.

"Are you gonna tell me what happened to your face?" Shenin asked.

"Let's just say never try to take a bottle of beer away from a drunk ex-Ranger and leave it at that," Jet said, grinning.

She'd been dodging questions all day about the nasty bruise on her cheek, and was praying she wouldn't run into Kashena, or Sebastian for that matter.

"So," Jet said, her tone even. "What's up with you?"

"What do you mean?" Shenin asked, on her guard immediately.

Jet raised an eyebrow at the tension she heard in Shenin's tone. "I mean, your girl came all the way from Washington, D.C. to see you, and that should have had you walking on cloud nine…" She let her voice trail off, as she canted her head. "But that's not what I've seen…"

Shenin blew her breath out in a sigh. Her time with Tyler had been a series of ups and downs. They'd had fun in Sacramento and San Francisco, but there'd been a few arguments and some tension. It was something their relationship was never devoid of anymore.

"There's just a lot going on," Shenin said, shaking her head.

"Like what?" Jet asked, knowing that Shenin was trying to play it off, but seeing that there was lot she wasn't saying.

"Well, there's the distance thing."

"Which she bridged to come here…" Jet said, her tone leading, because she sensed it wasn't what Shenin meant.

Shenin shook her head, her eyes downcast. "She can be right next to me and there's still distance between us," she said sadly.

Jet nodded. "So is that her, or is that you?" she asked.

Shenin looked back at Jet, surprised that she was asking, but realizing that Jet saw a lot more than she said most of the time.

"It's me, it's always me…" Shenin said, her tone self-effacing.

Again Jet nodded. "Okay…" She tilted her head then. "Do you know why?"

Shenin pressed her lips together, nodding.

"Do you want to talk to me about it?" Jet asked then, her voice gentle.

She saw Shenin's lips tremble, and knew that this woman desperately needed someone to talk to. To Jet's way of thinking, she should be talking to Tyler, but she assumed there was a reason she couldn't or wouldn't talk to her. Leaning forward, Jet put her hand over Shenin's, her look pained.

"Dev, you gotta get it out," she said, her tone still gentle. "Or it'll eat you alive."

Shenin let out a soft sob, and Jet immediately moved to hug her. Shenin let Jet hold her, feeling like she was doing the wrong thing, but also feeling like Jet might be the only person she could talk to at this point. Jet pulled back, looking down at Shenin.

"Talk," she said simply.

Shenin swallowed convulsively a couple of times, looking down at the table, her fingernails picking at the tablecloth.

"I have PTSD," she said simply.

"Okay..." Jet said. "Tell me what happened."

Shenin drew in a deep breath, still picking at the tablecloth. "I was with a team sent to Iraq to set up a post... We were taken hostage by ISIS members..."

Jet closed her eyes slowly, a cold feeling in the pit of her stomach. Shenin saw Jet's expression, knowing that Jet knew exactly how that would have felt.

"Were you hurt?" Jet asked quietly.

Shenin blinked a couple of times, then she held out her right arm, touching the small scar on her upper arm. "Gunshot to the arm," she said, shrugging.

Jet narrowed her eyes, sensing more. "What happened next?"

"They held us for almost two weeks…" Shenin said, her focus once again on the tablecloth.

Jet took out a cigarette, lighting it and handing it to Shenin and then lighting one for herself.

"Okay…" Jet said, waiting for the rest.

"And they traded us back to the Air Force," Shenin said.

"And that's the story that Ty knows," Jet said, her tone matter of fact.

Shenin pressed her lips together and nodded.

"So what really happened?" Jet asked.

Shenin bit her lower lip, her eyes down, her body tense.

"Dev?" Jet queried, waving away the waitress who was approaching the table.

Shenin started shaking her foot in subdued agitation, but Jet just waited.

After a long few minutes, Shenin whispered, "Let's just say that not all of the ISIS members were… ah, gentlemen."

Jet closed her eyes, grimacing. "Jesus…" she breathed. Opening them, she looked at Shenin, she could see that Shenin was doing her best not to cry. "You were raped," she said, her tone even.

Shenin blew out a jagged breath, nodding her head.

"And Tyler doesn't know," Jet said.

Shenin shook her head, tears dropping onto her clenched hand sitting in her lap.

"You have to tell her, Shenin…" Jet told her, her voice hoarse with emotion.

"I can't," Shenin said, shaking her head vehemently.

"You have to," Jet said, her tone stronger now.

Shenin lifted her head, her eyes shining. "You don't understand," she said.

"Tell me what I don't understand," Jet said, her voice calmer, sensing that Shenin needed to say everything.

"Tyler was supposed to go on that mission," Shenin said, focusing on the lit cigarette in her hand. "She got pulled at the last minute. She already feels like shit that this happened when she was supposed to be there. If I tell her this… it'll kill her…" She said the last shaking her head.

"Shenin, not knowing what's going on inside your head is going to kill her, it'll just take more time…" Jet said.

"You think I should just tell her this?" Shenin asked, anger in her voice now.

"Yeah," Jet said, her look direct.

"How would you feel?" Shenin asked then. "If it were Fadiyah?"

"It was Fadiyah," Jet said. "One of them was about to rape her when I got there."

"Yeah, but you got there," Shenin snapped. "What if you hadn't? What if you'd been too late?"

Jet looked back at Shenin, shocked by her sudden anger, but also shocked by what she'd just said. She was right, she'd gotten there in time. This was Tyler's wife, the woman she loved, who had been violated... And she hadn't gotten there in time...

Shenin saw the moment it clicked in Jet's head, and she saw in Jet's eyes the devastation she knew she'd see in Tyler's if she ever told her what had really happened; only it would be ten times worse. Tyler had always felt responsible for Shenin, since the day that they had met at Nellis Air Force Base in Las Vegas. Tyler had looked out for her.

"Oh my God..." Jet said, her tone reflecting the absolute horror of the situation.

She looked at Shenin then, seeing more shadows in her eyes.

"There's more isn't there?" Jet asked, feeling slightly sick again and desperately wanting a drink instead of lunch.

Shenin nodded. "About a month and a half after I got back, I kept feeling sick..."

Jet grimaced, knowing what she was going to say.

"I took a test... It was positive... I was pregnant," Shenin said, looking sick.

"What did you do?" Jet asked, knowing the answer.

"Well, I'd just been assigned here, so when I got here I went down to Mexico and took care of it."

"In Mexico?" Jet asked, shocked.

"I didn't want the Air Force to have record of it."

"But... Mexico?" Jet asked, imagining all kinds of unsanitary back alleys where things like abortions were performed.

Shenin shrugged. "I just wanted it out."

Jet winced at her words, shaking her head.

"How are you dealing with all of this?" Jet asked.

Shenin held up the cigarette in her hand.

"Are you talking to anyone?" Jet asked then.

"I'm seeing a PTSD counselor," Shenin said evenly.

"But you haven't told the counselor this, have you?" Jet asked, knowing the answer.

"She'd tell the Air Force," Shenin said.

Jet drew in a deep breath. "And what happens if this ruins your marriage?"

Shenin shook her head. "If it's going to, it's going to. I'm not going to add to Tyler's guilt."

"She loves you, Shenin." Jet said.

"I know," she said, "and that's why I can't do this to her. It's bad enough that she wasn't there. I can't tell her this... I can't."

"So you'd let her think that you stopped loving her?" Jet asked.

"If that's what it takes," Shenin said. "But I'm really hoping I can just get past it at some point and we can get back to being good."

"How's that going?" Jet asked, her look pointed.

"Shut it, Jet," Shenin said, giving her a narrowed look.

"Uh-huh," Jet said, nodding.

Later that evening, Jet was sitting in her backyard, smoking and drinking a beer.

"You managed to avoid me all day…" Sebastian said, standing in the doorway of the rear sliding door.

Jet blew her breath out, shaking her head.

Sebastian walked over to her, seeing the dark bruise on her cheek and grimacing. He hadn't been responsible for a mark on a woman like that since he and Kashena had their first meeting. That had been a fair fight, however, this had not.

He reached out to touch Jet's cheek and she quickly yanked her head away from him.

"Don't!" she snapped, her eyes narrowed.

Sebastian looked at her, his look pained. Blowing his breath out, he moved to sit down in the chair across from her.

"Jet, I'm sorry." Jet didn't look at him, she simply nodded, her knee moving in agitation.

"You know I didn't mean to do that," he said, his tone still apologetic.

"Yeah," Jet said, still not raising her eyes to his.

"But I was pissed at you," he said.

Jet nodded, her eyes finally meeting his, the look in them hurt.

Sebastian closed his eyes slowly, he'd let his jealousy over Ashley damage his relationship with Jet and he had no idea how to fix it. Jet was a convoluted mass of contradictions; he couldn't read her like he could Kashena. When he thought he knew something about this girl, he was wrong. Worst of all, he really cared for her, but had no idea what to do with those feelings. He'd expressed them by following her to Iraq and covering her. Now, back in the real world, he had no idea what to do. And now they were farther apart than ever and there didn't seem to be an easy path back.

In the end he left the house feeling no better than when he'd arrived, in fact he felt worse having seen the damage he'd done both internally and externally. Back at the apartment, Ashley was waiting for him.

She was sitting on his bed, reading a book. He walked in, kicked off his shoes and climbed onto the bed. Lying on his stomach and putting his head in her lap, he wrapped his arms around her.

Ashley set her book aside, her look surprised by his action. She put her hands in his hair, stroking it and looking down at him.

"It went that badly?" she asked him, having known where he was going.

He nodded, looking miserable.

"She wouldn't talk to you?"

"What little she did say was enough," he said.

Ashley grimaced, she knew that Jet was really hurt by the whole incident with Sebastian and she felt bad, because she knew it was all her fault. She decided to try and talk to Jet about it.

***

"You'll be fine, babe..." Jet said, looking over at Fadiyah who was wringing her hands nervously in the passenger seat.

They were driving through the local college campus. It was Fadiyah's first day in college and she was terrified.

"I could start next semester," Fadiyah said, her tone hopeful.

"Babe, it's only a student visa if you're using it, and if they find out you're not in school they could deport you immediately."

"Okay," Fadiyah said, nodding. They'd discussed this at length a few times, but she was very nervous about going to an American college.

Jet reached across the console and held Fadiyah's hand, squeezing it gently. "It'll be okay, babe, I promise."

Jet parked in the visitor lot and walked around the car to open Fadiyah's door, glancing around as she did. She could see various curious looks at her car. She knew the Maserati always drew attention, she was used to it. Fadiyah got out of the car, putting her trembling hand in Jet's to get out. Feeling bad about how nervous she was, Jet pulled Fadiyah to her, hugging her close.

"It will be okay," she said again, into Fadiyah's ear.

Fadiyah nodded, taking a deep breath, inhaling Jet's scent and trying to hold onto her very essence to get her through this first day. Jet pulled back, looking down at Fadiyah.

"You okay?" she asked.

Fadiyah nodded again.

They walked toward where Fadiyah's first class was located. Jet noted a man, very obviously Middle Eastern, looking at Fadiyah. His eyes first looking at her face, then dropping to her hand clasped in Jet's, then he looked at Jet. He was obviously very displeased with what he was seeing.

"He is Iraqi," Fadiyah said, her tone tremulous.

"And that's his problem," Jet said quietly to Fadiyah.

"He is angry." Fadiyah said then, surprised by the look on the man's face.

"Madha tafeal?" the man asked harshly in Arabic. "'Ant ear eayilatuk!" He was asking her what she was doing, and exclaiming that she shames her family.

He stepped menacingly toward Fadiyah, and Jet immediately pulled Fadiyah behind her, stepping in front of her and between her and the man.

"I'm going to tell you once to back up," Jet said to the man, her tone all cop.

"You are not Iraqi! You should not be with her, you are a filthy creature!"

"See, now you're just pissing me off," Jet said, narrowing her eyes. "Hi taht himayat baladi," she told him, telling him that Fadiyah was under her protection. "Now back the fuck off…"

The man looked shocked at her perfectly accented Arabic, but it was a momentary pause. He actually had the temerity to raise his hand as if he was going to hit Jet. He didn't even have half a chance to finish whatever thought he was doing before Jet had him on the ground, with the hand he'd raised up behind his back and her knee on the back of his shoulder.

"Oh, I'm sorry, did I forget to mention that I'm a cop and it's never wise to threaten one?" Jet asked, her tone mild.

"I have rights…" the man gritted out.

Leaning down, Jet spoke into the man's ear. "So does she you dumb fucker…" she growled. "Violate them again, and I'll throw your ass in jail. Are we clear?"

The man tried to fight against Jet's hold. She lifted his arm higher on his back, making him subside quickly.

"Are... we... clear?" Jet asked him again.

"Yes!" he yelped.

"Good," Jet said, letting go of his arm and moving to stand.

She glanced around noting that a lot of people were staring. She felt Fadiyah's hand in hers immediately, and felt the girl standing close behind her. The man got up off the ground and quickly walked away. Jet watched him go, and continued watching until he was out of sight. Then she turned to look at Fadiyah.

"Well, that was fun," She said, beaming.

"You have a strange sense of fun," Fadiyah said, giving her an odd look.

Jet grinned. "Yeah, I know. Come on, let's find your class."

With Fadiyah safely in class, Jet made her way into the office, only to find Ashley waiting for her. It had been a week since Ashley had moved in with Sebastian.

"Hey," Jet said, moving to hug Ashley. "What's up?"

Ashley looked cautiously at Jet for a long moment, which immediately put Jet on alert.

"What?" Jet asked when Ashley didn't say anything.

"I want to talk to you about Sebastian."

"Why?" Jet asked, moving to hook up her phone to her computer so she could turn her music on.

"Because I want this fixed between you two," Ashley said.

Jet looked over at Ashley, her look unreadable. "Why?" she asked again.

"Jet, don't be like that," Ashley said, her tone chiding.

"Look, its fine, we're fine, just leave it alone, okay?" Jet said, her tone even.

"Jet…" Ashley said, her voice trailing off as she gave Jet a searching look.

"Ash," Jet said her tone sharper now. "Just leave it alone."

This time it was Ashley that left feeling like she'd failed. She'd been afraid to push Jet, not wanting to irritate her.

***

Shenin sat completely still, her hand on the ground next to her. She almost held her breath as she waited. Suddenly she felt the lightest touch of a whisker on her hand. She didn't move, she knew if she did at that moment she'd lose her.

"It's okay…" she said so very softly it could barely be heard.

The whiskers got closer, she was sniffing her hand. Shenin smiled as she felt the little nose on her arm.

"It's okay, baby…" she said then, still very softly.

The little Chihuahua moved closer, wanting the treat she was holding in her left hand that she held in her lap. She waited with endless patience, and eventually the little dog did just as she'd hoped and moved to get up into her lap to take the treat.

Shenin had spent a half an hour just working with this dog to try and get her to be less fearful. It made her feel good to help the little dogs find their way. She felt like every time she was able to make a dog less fearful of people, she helped them get closer to finding a home.

"You are so good at that," Skyler said shaking her head in amazement.

"It just takes patience," Shenin said, smiling.

"I guess," Skyler said, shaking her head.

Shenin had been talking to Skyler about her work with the dogs at the local animal shelter, and Skyler had been interested in checking it out. She'd finally gotten a chance to see Shenin in action. Shenin liked to work with the most timid of the dogs at the shelter. Usually that meant the smallest dogs, but there were times when there was a big dog that needed help. Shenin didn't feel comfortable with big dogs, but she thought someone like Skyler would be perfect. She had a natural affinity with dogs, and had worked tirelessly with her dog, Benny, training him.

Skyler had watched Shenin work with the tiny Chihuahua and was amazed at the change in the dog after Shenin had worked with her. Shenin had told her it was what she did to help cope with the PTSD. She'd shared the general story of her capture in Iraq, and Skyler had told her about the helicopter crash that had affected her so strongly. It was part of the bond that they shared and what had allowed them to become good friends.

Later that day Shenin was just walking into her apartment when her phone rang, she saw that it was Tyler.

"Hi," she said, answering the phone smiling.

"How was the shelter?" Tyler asked, smiling at her end.

"It was good," she answered, moving to pet Muffit who was waiting patiently at her feet. "Skyler came down today," she said then.

"She did?" Tyler asked, doing her best not to feel that pang of concern.

"Yeah, I think she's going to start working with some of the bigger dogs," Shenin said, sounding excited.

"Well, I'm sure that'll be good, to help some of them," Tyler said, still feeling somewhat jealous that this was all happening while she wasn't there.

"Oh yeah," Shenin said, moving to stand up and walk into the kitchen. "Some of the pit bulls are really scared a lot of the time, and that makes them really hard to adopt out," she was saying as she reached for a pot to boil water in. She had to stretch to get it and suddenly felt a sharp pain in her abdomen, and gasped in response.

"Shen?" Tyler queried, hearing the gasp.

"It's okay," Shenin said, rubbing her stomach and moving to lean against the counter. "Must have pulled something at the gym this morning," she said, grinning.

"Maybe take it a little easier on the workouts, huh?" Tyler said.

"It's hard to do that with Natalia. She's a worse task master than Vanessa up in Alaska was!"

"Well, try, sheesh," Tyler said, grinning.

Shenin grimaced at her end, the pain wasn't subsiding.

"Hey, I'm gonna go," Shenin said. "I need to eat something and I'm meeting the girls later."

"Okay," Tyler said, once again feeling the sadness that came every time Shenin seemed to be pulling away.

They hung up a couple of minutes later. Shenin moved to sit down, trying to breathe through the pain in her stomach. After a few minutes it seemed to get better. She got up and took some Motrin, then went about cooking a quick meal.

Three hours later she met the group at the club. Her abdomen still hurt a bit, but it wasn't as sharp. She had a few drinks and felt even better. At one point she'd gone to the bathroom and noticed blood. Thinking she'd started her period, she put in a tampon and thought nothing more about it.

An hour later, she was dancing with the girls, with Jet standing nearby; it was her 'shift' as Jet and Skyler jokingly called it. She started to feel dizzy and put her hand out grabbing Jet's hand.

"What's wrong... Dev!" Jet yelled as Shenin collapsed.

Jet caught her in her arms, taking her down to the floor as Skyler and Jericho rushed to them.

"What happened?" Skyler asked.

"I don't know. She grabbed my hand and then she just dropped..." Jet said, moving to pick Shenin up. She was out cold.

"She looks really pale," Jericho said.

Skyler moved to check Shenin's pulse.

"It's fast," Skyler said, looking at Jet.

"Let's go," Jet said moving toward the doors to the club even as Skyler pulled out her phone calling 911.

Five minutes later an ambulance came. Jet got in the ambulance with Shenin, the rest of the group was going to follow. Shenin had not regained consciousness.

At the hospital, Shenin was taken in immediately; the EMTs had said her blood pressure was low, and that they thought there was some kind of internal bleeding.

It was another hour before they came out to talk to the group that had gathered. They couldn't tell them much, but did ask for contact information for a family member. Jet gave them Tyler's name and her cell phone number.

Tyler was asleep when her cell phone rang.

"Hancock," she answered automatically assuming it would be the base.

"Tyler Hancock?" said the voice on the other end of the line.

Tyler went cold. It was the same officious tone she'd heard when Shenin had been in the car accident. "Yes?"

"Ma'am, we have your wife here at Cedars Sinai, and she needs emergency exploratory surgery. She is unconscious so cannot give consent. Do we have yours?"

"Yes, of course, but what happened?"

"Ma'am, your wife was brought in via ambulance. She collapsed at a local club this evening."

Tyler had to breathe slowly so she wouldn't scream at the person on the other end of the line. "Okay, I'll get there as soon as I can, but I'm in Maryland."

"We will proceed with surgery," the woman said.

"Yes, please, do whatever you can or need to, thank you," Tyler said, dying to get off the phone so she could get ahold of an airline.

Chapter 7

Six hours after the phone call, Tyler, dressed in her BDUs, strode into the hospital and straight up to Jet.

"What the hell happened?!" she practically shouted. It was the question that had been screaming in her mind for the last six hours.

Skyler and Jericho immediately moved to Jet's side, seeing how intense Tyler was and worried she'd take it out on Jet.

"We were at the club," Jet said, glancing at Skyler and Jericho. "She just collapsed; we have no idea what happened."

"She said something about pulling a muscle earlier when I talked to her," Tyler said, her mind racing.

Jet shook her head. "She didn't say anything about that tonight."

Tyler went over to the nurses station to let her know that she was there and wanted to know her wife's condition. The nurse said she would have the doctor come talk to her.

Five minutes later the doctor walked out.

"Mrs. Hancock?" he queried.

"Yes," Tyler said, standing at near attention in her tension. "How is she?"

"Your wife is resting comfortably," he told her.

Tyler blew her breath out in relief, nodding her head. "What was the problem?"

"Well, your wife had an internal bleed from a perforated uterus. There was some very abnormal scarring on her uterus, has she had surgery recently?"

Tyler looked surprised and completely mystified. Behind her Jet closed her eyes, knowing exactly what the problem had been from, but knowing that Tyler wouldn't know that.

"No, she hasn't had any surgeries recently," Tyler said. "What kind of surgery are we talking about?"

"It's hard to say," the doctor said. "I'm checking with my colleagues to see if there would be any other reason for this type of scarring. In the meantime, let me take you back to see her."

"Thanks." Tyler nodded, glancing back at the group and nodding to them in appreciation for their being there. "I'll let her know you're all here."

As Tyler walked away, Skyler elbowed Jet.

"You know something, don't you?" Skyler asked Jet.

Jet nodded, watching Tyler go through the doors. "But it's not my story to tell," she said, looking unhappy.

In the room, Tyler walked over to Shenin's bedside. Shenin's eyes were closed. Reaching over, Tyler took Shenin's hand in hers and noticed they were cold.

"We had to transfuse her," the doctor said. "She'll need to take it easy for a few days, but she should be just fine," he said, smiling, seeing the love on Tyler's face as she looked down at her wife.

"Thanks doc," Tyler said, smiling at the man.

The doctor left, and Tyler looked at Shenin, reaching over to brush a lock of hair off her cheek. Shenin opened her eyes.

"Ty?" she queried, then looked around her. "What happened?"

"You collapsed at the club," Tyler told her.

Shenin blinked a couple of times, looking like she was trying to remember.

"I remember dancing... Jet was standing guard as usual..." she said. "Then... I suddenly felt dizzy... That's the last thing I remember."

"Well, it sounds like that's probably when you collapsed," Tyler said, her look solicitous. "The doctor said that you were bleeding internally," she said, her tone pained. "He asked if you'd had any surgeries recently."

Shenin swallowed convulsively, but shrugged. "Why did he think that?"

"He said there was some strange scarring on your uterus..." Tyler said, noting Shenin's closed look suddenly. "Shen?" she asked. "What is it?"

Shenin closed her eyes. "Nothing, I'm just tired," she said, squeezing Tyler's hand gently.

Tyler looked back at her wife, knowing there was more to it than that, but not wanting to argue.

"Rest babe," she said, leaning over to kiss Shenin lightly on the lips.

Shenin nodded, keeping her eyes closed.

A couple of hours later when Shenin woke up she was surprised to see Jet standing next to the bed. Glancing over, she saw that Tyler wasn't there. Jet looked very circumspect.

"You need to tell her," Jet said to Shenin.

"No," Shenin said, shaking her head.

"You don't think she's trying to figure out how this happened?" Jet asked Shenin.

"I know," Shenin said. "Trust me, I've been married to her for four years, but I'm not telling her, so it's just going to have to be a mystery."

Jet did not look pleased. She shook her head slowly, thinking that Shenin was playing with fire and she was going to get both her and Tyler burned at the rate she was going. There was a part of Jet that wanted to tell Tyler everything, but she knew Shenin would never forgive her. The question was, what was love worth? It wasn't an easy answer.

Shenin saw the thoughts play across Jet's face, and sensed that Jet was trying to decide whether or not to tell Tyler.

"I can see what you're thinking," Shenin said, almost in a growl. "Don't do it. You have no idea what damage you'll cause."

"As opposed to the damage you're causing," Jet said, her tone matter of fact.

"That's my business," Shenin said.

Jet made a sound through her teeth, tilting her head, not saying anything, her eyes saying enough.

Shenin closed her eyes slowly. "Jet, please..." she said, her voice tremulous now. "You can't... please..."

"You need to tell her," Jet said, her tone brooking no argument.

"Tell who?" Tyler asked, as she walked into the room carrying some coffee, her look going between them. "Tell who?" she repeated when neither Jet nor Shenin spoke.

"No one," Shenin said, her look at Jet pointed. "Jet's just being a mother hen."

"Yeah, that's me," Jet said, tight-lipped.

Tyler once again looked between the two, her look suspicious.

"What's going on?" Tyler asked.

"Nothing," Shenin said.

Tyler looked at Jet. "Jet?" she queried.

Jet held up her hands. "I'm gonna go get my car," she said, nodding toward the door.

Tyler followed Jet out of the room.

"Jet," Tyler called, as Jet strode down the hallway.

Jet stopped, grimacing while still facing away from Tyler. Then she turned, her face expressionless.

"Yeah?" she asked.

Tyler's blue eyes searched Jet's face. "Is there something I need to know?"

Jet narrowed her eyes slightly, but shook her head. "No," she said, her tone far from convincing.

Tyler took a deep breath, expelling it slowly. "And this doesn't have anything to do with what we talked about?" she asked, gesturing to the hospital as a whole.

"No, absolutely not," Jet said, her tone strong this time.

Tyler nodded, her look still quizzical, but she could tell she wasn't going to get anything out of Jet.

"Thanks for being there for her," Tyler said, feeling a little sick that she was telling another woman that, when she knew damned good and well she should have been there for her wife... again.

Jet could see the look in Tyler's eyes, knowing exactly what she was thinking. She nodded, looking pained. She felt for Tyler, she knew what it would do to her to have to rely on someone else to take care of Fadiyah. The situation sucked completely.

Skyler drove Jet back to the club to get her car. Looking over at the other woman she could see that Jet was unhappy.

"So," Skyler said, her tone leading. "What was that back there?" she asked. "You know more about this situation than you're saying, don't you?"

Jet nodded, looking anguished.

"Spill," Skyler said.

"Can't," Jet said, shaking her head.

"Sure you can," Skyler said. "You know you can trust me."

"It's not me that needs to trust you."

"Shenin?" Skyler asked.

Jet nodded.

"Okay, so there's obviously something that you know that Tyler doesn't," Skyler said, her mind turning over everything she knew about Shenin and Tyler. "Have to do with anything here?" she asked, circling her hand, to indicate Los Angeles.

Jet shook her head.

"Back East?" Skyler asked.

Again, Jet shook her head.

"So, Iraq," Skyler said. Jet gave her a look that told her she had hit it. "Okay, so… something happened in Iraq that Tyler doesn't know about?"

"Yep," Jet said, her tone even.

Skyler nodded her head, her mind racing. What could have happened that would make Shenin not want to tell Tyler? It could have had to do with the team that went over… Shenin didn't seem like the cheating type, so Skyler doubted that was it… Skyler knew that Tyler was chewed up with guilt about not being there when Shenin was taken hostage… But Shenin had been lucky only getting a gunshot wound to the arm… unless… Then it clicked.

"Oh fuck…" Skyler said, her tone telling Jet that she'd made the connections.

"You're telling me…" Jet said, relieved that she hadn't had to actually tell Skyler anything, therefore not having betrayed Shenin's trust, in a roundabout way.

"But what would that have to do with…" Skyler started to say, thinking about what the doctor had told Tyler about the perforated uterus. Then the next thought struck.

She thought she was going to be sick. She actually needed to pull her car over to the curb for a minute as a wave of nausea hit her. Jet looked over at Skyler and knew that she'd figure it all out now. She also knew what Skyler was doing in her head; the exact thing that Jet had done. She put Fadiyah in that situation and thinking about how she'd feel if she was in Tyler's position.

"Ignorance is definitely bliss here…" Skyler said, her tone tremulous. "But this thing tonight…"

"I know," Jet said, her tone grave.

"If that doctor figures it out…" Skyler said, her voice trailing off as she looked over at Jet.

"Then Shenin's not going to have a choice but to tell Tyler."

"You really think so?" Skyler asked, her tone speculative.

"Jesus. You don't think she'd let her think that… No…" Jet said, wondering if Shenin would go so far as to let Tyler think she'd cheated on her with a man and gotten pregnant in order to protect Tyler's pride. Jet didn't want to believe Shenin would do that.

Neither of them knew for sure.

"Tyler overheard me telling Dev that she needed to tell Ty…"

"Seriously?" Skyler asked.

"Yeah," Jet said.

"And how did you explain that?"

"Dev told her it was nothing," Jet said.

"Son of a bitch… You do realize how dangerous a spot you're in right now, right?" Skyler asked Jet then. "'Cause you know she thinks something is going on…"

Jet gave a short humorless laugh. "Ya think?" she asked sarcastically.

"And she'd take you apart before you even had a chance to explain…" Skyler said, shaking her head.

"I know," Jet said.

"Jesus, Jet…" Skyler said, worried for her friend now.

Jet simply nodded, knowing she was in a bad spot with no really good way out of it.

"Have you told Fadiyah anything?" Skyler asked.

"No," Jet said, looking worried, "but I'm thinking I'm going to need to tell her something."

"Make it the truth," Skyler said, her tone strong.

Jet blew her breath out, nodding her head. Cat had taken Fadiyah back to Jet's house earlier that night. Fadiyah had school in the morning and Jet didn't want her out too late so she'd miss school. Fadiyah was carrying an over-full class schedule to do some catching up.

Jet walked into the house at three that morning. She ended up out in her backyard smoking. Fadiyah found her there an hour later.

"Jet?" Fadiyah queried worriedly. "Is Shenin okay?"

"Yeah," Jet said, nodding. "She's gonna be fine."

Fadiyah nodded, looking relieved. Sitting down across from Jet she shivered in the cool early morning air. Jet saw it and stood up taking off her jacket and putting it around Fadiyah's shoulders.

"I need to tell you some stuff," Jet said then, lighting another cigarette.

Fadiyah looked worried for a moment.

"No, babe, nothing bad, okay?" Jet said, reaching over with one hand to touch Fadiyah's cheek. "I just need to catch you up on some stuff, so that if the shit hits the fan you won't be blindsided, okay?"

Fadiyah looked confused by some of the metaphors, but Jet went ahead and told her what was happening with Tyler and Shenin and how she fit into it. When she finished the story, Fadiyah was in tears.

"That is so terrible," Fadiyah said, shaking her head sadly. "I am so sorry for Shenin."

Jet nodded. "Yeah it's really rough."

Fadiyah regarded Jet for a long moment. "What she asked you… about if you had not gotten there in time for me…"

Jet nodded slowly, waiting for the rest of the question.

"What did you say?" Fadiyah asked.

Jet shook her head. "I couldn't answer," she said. "I don't know what I would have done… It's beyond the scope of my imagination as to how I would've reacted. Just the idea of it…" Her voice was halting, and finally trailed off as she shook her head, her look devastated.

Fadiyah reached her hand out, touching Jet's face, her expression one of complete devotion. "That is why I love you," she said, her voice soft. "Because you are so amazing."

Jet looked back at her. "I'm just me, babe," she said, shaking her head.

"And who you are is amazing Jet Blue Mathews," Fadiyah said, moving to sit on Jet's lap, putting her arms around her neck and staring down into her eyes.

Jet reached up, bringing Fadiyah's face down to hers, kissing her lips. She then moved to stand, picking the smaller girl up in her arms and carried her inside and up to their bedroom where she made love to her until it was time for Fadiyah to get ready for school. They were both a little tired that day, but it didn't matter to either of them.

***

Shenin was released from the hospital the evening following her admission. Tyler drove Shenin back to the apartment and got her set up in bed to rest. She got Shenin some dinner and took Muffit for a walk. After they ate, Tyler sat next to her on the bed and they watched TV. Tyler put her arm around Shenin's shoulder and Shenin snuggled against Tyler sighing softly. It felt so good to be almost normal at that moment, neither of them wanted to spoil it with questions and issues.

Shenin fell asleep lying against Tyler. Tyler carefully moved to lay Shenin down, then got up to take a quick shower and put on sweat pants and a tank top, before lying down next to Shenin carefully. Shenin immediately snuggled against Tyler's warmth, and Tyler did her best to savor every moment.

Tyler knew there was something going on and she knew that at some point she was going to need to deal with the reality of it. She didn't know if it had to do with Jet, or someone else in the group. What she did know was that there was something that Jet Mathews knew that she didn't and she didn't like it at all. She really hoped that her trust in Jet hadn't been misplaced, but something told her it wasn't. Not knowing was driving her crazy.

Tyler was asleep when she felt Shenin jolt awake. Looking down she saw a fearful look in Shenin's eyes as she blinked a few times to try and wake up.

"Babe?" Tyler queried, worried.

Shenin was breathing heavily, her hand clenching and unclenching at Tyler's shoulder.

"Shen?" Tyler said, her eyes searching Shenin's face. "Honey, you with me?"

Shenin looked at her then, her eyes focusing. Then she nodded.

"Nightmare?" Tyler asked.

Shenin blew her breath out, nodding.

Tyler nodded, waiting, her hands stroking Shenin's arm and shoulder soothingly. "Do you want to tell me about it?"

Shenin shook her head. "It's... I can't really even remember it now."

"Okay..." Tyler said, feeling like Shenin was lying, but not willing to call her on it.

Shenin went back to sleep a little while later. Tyler lay awake wondering what was happening, why Shenin was so closed off from her that she was outright lying to her now.

The next day Shenin didn't mention the nightmare, but that night she woke with a start again and a yelp this time when Tyler touched her shoulder.

"Jesus!" Tyler exclaimed. "Babe, it's me."

Shenin nodded, breathing heavily and grasping at Tyler's arms.

"I suppose you don't want to tell me about this one either..." Tyler said, her tone flat. Even so, Shenin gave her sharp look, Tyler refused to take it back.

Shenin shook her head, putting her forehead against Tyler's chest. Tyler's lips tightened, even as she closed her eyes, fighting the desire to shake her wife. This was absolutely maddening and she didn't know how much more of it she could take. Shenin had slept most of the next day. Tyler had left to walk Muffit again, and had just come back into the apartment when she heard Shenin saying, "No" sounding upset. She moved toward the bedroom and saw that Shenin was lying on the bed her eyes still closed, but she was writhing, like she was trying to get away, her head moving back and forth.

Tyler moved to the side of the bed, and she reached out gently touching Shenin on the shoulder. She was stunned when Shenin's eyes flew open and Shenin literally backed up into a crouched position at the other side of the bed, her eyes extremely fearful.

"Jesus fucking Christ!" Tyler exclaimed, out of complete shock at Shenin's reaction.

She moved to sit on the bed reaching for Shenin, but Shenin threw her arms up in a 'hands off' gesture.

"Don't!" Shenin cried, her voice terrified.

"Shenin, it's me!" Tyler yelled, her voice strident because she had no idea what was going on and it terrified her.

Shenin's hands stayed up in a warding off gesture. "Please Ty, just don't, please…" she said, her voice breathless and trembling.

"Shenin, what the fuck is going on?" Tyler asked, her patience completely gone.

Shenin shook her head, putting her hand to head, her hand shaking like a leaf.

"No, you don't get to do that this time, Shenin," Tyler said, her tone sharp. "You're going to tell me what's going on and you're going to tell me right the fuck now."

Shenin shrank from her, curling her other arm around herself defensively.

"Jesus..." Tyler breathed, moving to take Shenin in her arms again.

Shenin jerked away, but Tyler grabbed her upper arms, trying to pull her back to her. Shenin shoved against Tyler, her hands pushing at Tyler's chest and shoulder.

"No!" Tyler yelled, trying to get through to her wife. "Shenin, stop it!" she yelled, tightening her hold on Shenin's arms as she did.

Shenin cried out when Tyler's hands tightened to the point of bruising. Shenin lashed out with one arm, breaking Tyler's hold and catching Tyler in the face with her fist. Tyler's head snapped back and she fell backward on the bed, catching herself with her arm.

"Are you fucking crazy?" Tyler yelled at Shenin.

Shenin had already curled back into herself then, her knees up to her chest, her face against her legs, her arms wrapped around them. Tyler stood staring at Shenin, unable to believe what had just happened. Blind fury took over and Tyler turned and walked out of the room.

She left the apartment, got into her rental car and drove straight to Jet's house. Jet was out front washing her car, she saw Tyler drive up and get out of the car. She'd turned to turn her radio down and turned back only to catch a fist in the face that threw her three feet backwards onto the ground. Because her ears were ringing, it took her a minute to hear what Tyler was screaming at her.

"...I fucking trusted you, what did you do to her?" Tyler was screaming.

"Jet!" Fadiyah exclaimed. She'd heard the screaming and had come out of the house.

Tyler's menacing look shifted to Fadiyah and that had Jet vaulting to her feet to put herself between Fadiyah and an extremely angry Tyler.

Jet held her hands up. "Tyler, calm the fuck down!" she yelled. She glanced over her shoulder at Fadiyah. "Babe, go back in the house."

"But Jet... you're bleeding," Fadiyah said, her tone plaintive.

"I'm okay," she said. "Please babe..." Fadiyah did as Jet asked and Jet looked back at Tyler.

"Tell me what happened..." Jet said calmly to Tyler, hoping to influence Tyler's mood.

"My wife is fucking terrified of me," Tyler snapped. "That's what fucking happened!"

Jet drew in a deep breath and blew it out slowly. "What happened?" Tyler looked back at Jet. "What the fuck don't I know, Jet?" she snapped.

Jet shook her head. "You need to ask Shenin that question," she said simply.

"I've asked Shenin that question and she's not answering me," Tyler said, her eyes narrowing dangerously. "And whereas it's spousal abuse to beat it out of her, it's not to beat it out of you."

Jet's chin came up. "Then come try," she said, her tone challenging.

To back up her challenge, she dropped one foot back in a fighter's stance, her hands down at her sides, her fingers working like they were itching for a fight.

"Is that it?" Tyler asked, her look sharp.

"Is that what?" Jet asked looking confused.

"You're gonna fight me for her?" Tyler asked, her tone taking on a haunted tinge.

Jet shook her head. "That's not it at all," she said, her tone sad.

"Then what the fuck is it!" Tyler yelled, her temper boiling.

Jet looked back at Tyler, seeing the pain the other woman was in and unable to take anymore.

"She should be telling you this…" Jet said, her voice gravelly with emotion.

"Please…" Tyler said, with so much pain in her voice that Jet knew she didn't have a choice.

"Come on," Jet said, gesturing with her head into the house.

Tyler followed her into the house. Jet stopped in the kitchen to get a bottle of tequila. Then she let Tyler out to the backyard, stopping long enough to kiss Fadiyah's lips softly, winking at her.

Jet sat down, lighting a cigarette and turning the stereo on. Tyler stood waiting. Jet gestured for her to sit down. After a long moment, Tyler finally did.

"You don't know everything about Iraq," Jet told Tyler.

"What don't I know?" Tyler asked, not surprised by Jet's statement.

Jet looked back at Tyler, her look pained. "The gunshot wound wasn't the only damage…"

Tyler looked back at Jet, her face serious. "Tell me…"

"She was raped," Jet said, knowing that beating around the bush would only make things worse.

Tyler looked faint suddenly, and she put her hand up to her face, her hand shaking. "Oh my God…" she said, her voice a sick whisper. She looked up at Jet then. "Why didn't she tell me?"

Jet looked back at Tyler for a long moment, her look saying *you know why.*

Tyler nodded, swallowing convulsively. "Because she knew I already felt like shit for not being there in the first place…"

Jet nodded. "That's not all of it though," she said then, knowing that Tyler needed to hear it all.

Tyler blew her breath out again, nodding, and waiting.

"After she got back…" Jet said, grimacing. "About a month and a half after…" she said, trying to lessen the impact. She knew the minute it clicked in Tyler's head.

Tyler's hand shot out to brace herself on the table as she groaned like a wounded animal. In truth it felt like someone had just reached in and ripped out her heart. She couldn't breathe. In her head all she could hear was the roaring sound of, *No!* ripping through her skull. Her breath came in ragged gasps as she did her best to cope with what she'd just heard. Then something else occurred to her. Her head snapped up.

"What did she do?" she asked Jet.

Jet looked back at Tyler seeing the complete anguish in Tyler's blue eyes, and knowing that things would never be the same for her. She felt so sick for her that it physically hurt.

"She went down to Mexico," Jet said. "She didn't want a record of it with an American hospital."

Tyler stood up, moving blindly to the side of the yard and fell to her knees throwing up. She knew then that it was what had caused the perforated uterus, and it was something that could have killed Shenin and she'd never have known any of it. The implications, the recriminations, the sheer pain of it had Tyler throwing up until she was seeing red in her bile.

Jet, who had moved to stand by Tyler, handed Tyler the bottle of tequila. Tyler took it gratefully, and drank a large swig. Jet put her hand out, to help Tyler up off the ground. Tyler took it with shaking hands. Walking back over to the chairs in the backyard, Jet got Tyler to sit down, and handed her the tequila bottle again. She pulled out her phone then, texting Skyler.

The message read: "Shit hit the fan, go get Shenin, bring her here."

Skyler texted back: "Holy shit, will do."

Skyler knocked on Shenin's apartment door. When Shenin didn't answer, Skyler tried the door and was surprised to find it unlocked. Walking inside, she heard a dog whining.

"Shenin?" she called, hearing the dog whine louder.

She walked into the kitchen and beheld a sight she'd never forget as long as she lived. Shenin was sitting on the floor of the kitchen, her legs out in front of her, leaning against a cabinet. Muffit was lying with her head on Shenin's leg, whining pitifully. There was blood everywhere around the two, and a knife lay next to Shenin. The blood was coming from her wrists which she had cut repeatedly.

"Fuck!" Skyler yelled, dropping to her knees and grabbing at a towel on the counter. She wrapped it around both of Shenin's wrists, holding it as tightly as she could.

With her other hand she checked for a pulse.

"Come on Dev, come on..." Skyler chanted, trying to check again and again for a pulse... "Don't do this... Don't do this..."

Pulling out her phone, she dialed 911. "I need an ambulance at ten twenty-one Pineview," she said when the dispatcher answered. "Eleven ninety-nine officer down, I need an ambulance right now!"

Technically Shenin wasn't an officer, but since she was working for a law enforcement agency, Skyler figured what the hell.

"Come on Shenin!" Skyler yelled. "Don't do this!" she yelled, tears in her eyes.

Muffit started licking Shenin's face, and then kept looking at Skyler who felt like everything was crashing in at that moment.

Skyler felt for a pulse again and got a flutter.

"That's it, Dev, come on!" Skyler yelled. "Come on!"

She didn't want to perform CPR, knowing that doing so could force more of Shenin's blood out of the cuts. She didn't want to do that, unless she had to. A light pulse was still a pulse.

"Come on, come on, come on..." she chanted, banging her head on the cabinet next to where Shenin's head was, just needing to keep feeling something.

The paramedics came in then and Skyler moved as they worked on Shenin. She almost passed out with relief when they said they had a pulse. They put Shenin on a gurney, and Skyler followed them out. She picked up Muffit, getting Shenin's blood on her, since Muffit's paws were covered in it. She didn't care. She needed Muffit as much as the dog needed her right then.

In the ambulance, Skyler texted Jet: "All bad, all bad, get to Sinai now!"

Jet got the text and closed her eyes slowly, would this ever stop getting worse? Walking over to where Tyler sat she leaned down.

"Ty, I hate to do this, but we gotta go."

"Go?" Tyler asked, her eyes glassy, she'd drunk half a bottle of tequila by this time.

"Yeah, we gotta go, it's Shenin…"

"What?" Tyler asked, all the color draining from her face.

"Stay with me, Ty! We gotta get to Sinai, and we gotta get there, now." Jet moved to get Tyler up, but Tyler moved with surprising agility for someone who was half drunk.

As they strode toward the door, Jet grabbed Fadiyah's hand. "We gotta go," she told the girl. Fadiyah nodded, following Jet and Tyler out the front door, turning to lock it.

Jet pulled out her phone. Dialing dispatch she said, "LAPD Officer, Badge number three five nine seven, I need an emergency police escort to Cedars Sinai, from the West Hills, have them meet me on 101 at Valley Circle Drive, blue Maserati, plate two Zebra Echo X-ray four give six, now!"

"Ten-four!" the dispatcher replied.

Even as she was talking on the phone she was starting the car and speeding out of her driveway. Two LAPD officers met them on the onramp to Highway 101, one took up a position in front of Jet and the other in the back, lights and sirens blaring and clearing the way all the way to Cedars. As they pulled into the emergency room area, Jet flipped the officers a salute, and jumped out of the car, as Tyler jumped out and ran inside. Jet helped Fadiyah out of the car, holding her hand as she strode after Tyler, praying that they weren't too late. Jet suspected exactly what had happened. Skyler confirmed it as they walked up.

"Is she still alive?" Jet asked.

"Barely," Skyler said. "She lost a lot of blood..."

"Damnit..." Jet said, gritting her teeth.

Tyler made her way into the emergency room, heedless of the security officer that was trying to stop her. He made the mistake of grabbing her shoulder and she grabbed his hand and flipped around, putting him on the ground without slowing a pace. Finally, she found the room where Shenin was, and she moved to her wife's side. She already knew what she was going to see, but it made her sick anyway.

Shenin lay looking so pale as the doctors worked on trying to repair the damage she'd caused to her wrists. They were infusing blood, and had tightly wrapped her wrists. Tyler moved to her wife's head, kissing her temple, her tears mingling with Shenin's hair.

"You can't leave me here, babe... You can't leave..." she said, her voice desperate. Then she moved closer. "Remember what you said to me in Germany? I'm saying it to you now, babe... I love you more than life itself and I will not lose you... Do you hear me? If you love me, you'll stay with me Shenin... There's nothing we can't get through... I love you... I love you... Stay with me... Stay with me..." Tyler continued talking to Shenin until she was hoarse. Shenin's pulse, which had been light and thready when Tyler had walked into the room, stabilized and grew stronger. "That's it babe, that's it... Fight for me... Come back to me... I love you so much... Stay with me babe... Please stay with me, I can't live without you..." Her voice was a harsh whisper by that time, and there wasn't a dry eye in the room, every nurse, even the doctor was teary by that time.

"We've got her back," the doctor finally said, putting her hand on Tyler's shoulder.

Tyler nodded, lowering her head to rest it against Shenin's.

Chapter 8

Sebastian and Ashley lay sleeping in the early hours of the morning. Sebastian lay on his back, Ashley on her side next to him with his right arm around her, holding her close. The vibrating of his phone woke him. Reaching over to the nightstand he picked it up, and looked at the text message. Chuckling softly he answered it and set the phone down on the bed next to him.

"Work?" Ashley mumbled tiredly.

"Another woman," he said, grinning.

Ashley promptly ripped his chest with her teeth. Sebastian laughed even as he shifted slightly.

"I'm kidding, babe, it was my sister," he told her.

Ashley looked up at him then. "How old is she?"

"Almost your age, twenty-nine," he said.

She nodded. "Does she still live up in Sacramento?"

"Yeah," he said. "She's a nurse now, which is why she has no concept of normal time."

"Normal time?" Ashley asked.

Sebastian glanced at the clock on the nightstand it was four thirty in the morning. "Yeah, like when normal people are awake."

"We're awake right now, does that make us strange?" Ashley asked, grinning.

"No, that makes us crazy," he said, picking up his phone and shifting to lie on his side facing her, wincing slightly as he did.

"Is your back still hurting?" she asked.

"Yeah…" he said, moving his neck around to stretch it as he put his phone on the nightstand behind her.

"You need to stop hurting yourself to get over this thing with Jet," she told him. She knew that he was going to the gym and over doing it on his work outs to try and get rid of the stress of his still tenuous relationship with Jet.

He looked down at her, his look searching. "Do you even talk to her these days?" he asked her.

Ashley pressed her lips together. "That's different."

"How's it different?" he asked her.

Ashley didn't answer at first, then she shrugged. "I'm not taking it out on myself physically."

"But you're not talking to one of your best friends," he said. "That's not normal, Ash. She's not pissed at you."

"I know, but I think she's being stubborn about being pissed at you, and I don't like it. She knows damned good and well that you didn't mean to hit her."

"I know she does, but she also knows that I was pissed at her, and I know that I was jealous as hell of her, so even I wonder if there was something to that exchange."

Ashley levered up on her elbow, looking down at him. "Why do you say that?"

He looked back at her for a long moment. "I was in a really dark place at that moment… I wasn't thinking straight."

"You don't hit women, Sebastian," Ashley said, knowing that to her very core.

"I threatened Kash that day too."

She looked back at him surprised. "You did?"

He nodded, looking somber.

"Wow…" she said, her voice reflecting the shock.

"Yeah," he said, nodding. "See my point?"

"I see why you think you might have meant it," Ashley said. "But I still say it's not you."

He narrowed his eyes slightly, as his phone buzzed again. Reaching over he picked it up and looked at the message, grinning.

"You need to see this one," he said, turning his phone around so she could read the message.

Ashley read the message out loud. "I need to meet the woman that finally captured my big brother."

She looked up at Sebastian, surprised. "Captured?"

"You're living with me, right?" he said, grinning.

"Yeah…" she said, her brows furrowed.

"Captured," he said.

"Okay…" she said, still not looking sure of the word. "So what about your mom, is she still in Sacramento?"

"Yeah, she finally remarried a couple of years ago," he said, grinning.

"What?" she asked, noting the grin. "You don't like him?"

Sebastian shrugged. "Doesn't matter to me, what's important is that he's afraid of me."

Ashley looked back at him surprised, then understood. "Because of your dad," she said simply.

"Exactly," Sebastian said, nodding.

"But is your mom happy?" she asked.

"I suppose, she's happy enough."

"That doesn't sound that good…" Ashley said.

"It is what it is, babe. Sometimes you don't get blissfully happy, some people are okay with happy enough."

"Are you?" she asked, surprised by his statement.

He looked back at her for a long moment, his look considering. "No," he said simply, "I want it all."

Ashley smiled at him, liking that he was so honest.

His phone buzzed again, this time it was an email. She handed him his phone. He read the email nodding and then set it aside again.

"Got an air op this morning," he said, stretching. "With Jet and Sky as it happens."

"Really?" Ashley asked.

"Yep," he said, nodding. "Of course I'm on the ground and they're in the air, but…" he said, his voice trailing off as he grinned.

"Maybe you can do a post-operation beer…" Ashley said.

Sebastian looked back at her, his eyes narrowed. "You're scheming…" he told her.

"Am I?" she said innocently, as she blinked.

He shook his head. "To think I thought you were so sweet and innocent…" he said, his tone wistful.

Ashley laughed. "Like you'd want that for long!"

He grinned, she did know him, and he got bored with sweet and innocent pretty fast. It was her emerging wild side that was holding him fast, at least that's what he was telling himself.

"So what time do you have to get up?" she asked him.

"'Bout six, why?" he asked.

Ashley pushed him to his back, her body moving to cover his seductively, kissing him as she did.

"Mmm…" he murmured against her lips, even as his hands slid over her back, pressing her closer to him.

They kissed for a few very heated minutes, then she slid down over him, causing both of them to gasp loudly, even as they began to move together. Within minutes they were both crying out, his lips covering hers, his hands strong on her hips.

Afterwards, he shifted, wincing slightly.

"Oh babe, I'm sorry!" Ashley said. "I forgot your back… I'm sorry…"

"It's okay," he said, with a grin, as he used his forearm to lever himself up. Holding her to him with the other, he shifted back to his side, his body still inside hers. "It was definitely worth it," he said, with a wink.

"Mmm… I love when you do that…" she said, sighing.

"What?" he asked, settling comfortably again.

"Use all that strength to keep me right here," she said, lowering her head to kiss his chest.

He looked back at her, his eyes half closed. He liked that she said things like that; she didn't take anything for granted, and he liked that about her too.

Ashley moved to lie on her side next to Sebastian, glancing up at him as she did.

"So, would you mind if I texted your sister?" she asked him.

"No," he said, surprising her with his answer, "her number's in my phone."

Ashley reached over to pick up his phone and hers at the same time

"It's locked," she told him.

"Seven nine seven eight," he said.

Ashley looked back at him shocked.

"What?" he asked, seeing her disbelief.

Ashley shook her head, as she copied his sister's phone number into her phone to send a text.

"I'm just surprised that you gave me your passcode that easily," She said.

Sebastian grinned; he'd surprised himself with that one too. "I don't have anything to hide, Ash."

Ashley nodded, not looking at him.

He put his finger under her chin, tilting her face back up to his. "You know I was kidding about that other women comment, right?"

Ashley bit her lip and nodded uncertainly.

He leaned forward kissing her lips, then pulled back looking down into her eyes. "You're the only woman I'm seeing, the only one."

Ashley did her best not to look exceedingly pleased by this news. Even so, Sebastian saw it in her eyes.

"What's your sister's name?" she asked, noting that he just has "Sis" listed on his phone.

"Juliet," he told her.

Ashley began tapping out a message, and then she grimaced.

"What?" he asked, seeing her grimace.

"Hi, I'm Ashley, your brother's… uh… what do I say? Roommate?" she asked.

"How about girlfriend?" he said.

"Am I your girlfriend?" she asked him, her look flickering with uncertainty again.

"What part of *only woman I'm seeing* don't you get?" he asked, grinning. "I'd give you my class ring, but the only one I have is my Ranger one and I think it'll be a little bit big…"

"Stop it!" she said laughing.

Sebastian chuckled. "Seriously though, I definitely consider you my girlfriend," he said, his look earnest.

"You didn't even ask me to go steady…" she said, her grin sly.

"I think they call it 'going out' now," he said.

"Like on a date?" she asked, looking perplexed.

"Yeah, but that's how they ask someone to be exclusive."

"And you know this how?" she asked, her look quizzical.

Sebastian looked back at her, his grin roguish. "I think I'm gonna plead the fifth on that one."

"Oh, no…" she said, shaking her head, grinning. "How young do you date them Sebastian? Geeze! Are they even legal?"

Sebastian smiled wickedly. "Yes, they're always legal."

"Do I hear 'just barely' in that sentence?" she asked her look playful.

"Hey, legal is legal, babe," he said, his tone playful too.

"Uh-huh…" she murmured, giving him a sidelong glance.

He simply smiled back at her, his eyes sparkling mischievously.

They lay together for a while; she rested her head against his chest, breathing in the scent of him. The man smelled so damned good all of the time! She felt a shiver of desire go through her again; she never could get enough of him. She remembered something she'd read recently about controlling her body 'for her man's pleasure.' Remembering what the article said, her head still against his chest, she concentrated on her lower region muscles. She felt an immediate response from his body, and heard him draw in a sharp breath.

"Jesus…" he breathed against her hair, his hands on her skin flexing.

She continued, feeling him grow more and more excited, and the fact that she was exciting him this way, excited her. He started to shift.

"No," she said, looking up at him. "Don't move…" she said, her tone both commanding and husky.

His eyes stared back into hers, she could almost feel the heat from them as they bore into hers. She continued her ministrations, actually feeling him throbbing inside her. Moments later they were both crying out. His hands grasped at her, pressing her closer, his shout rumbling through his chest as she felt such a deep, intense orgasm she was almost light-headed when it subsided.

"Oh... my... God..." he gasped, his words measured as he tried to catch his breath. "Where the hell did that come from?" Ashley chuckled, still breathing heavily herself. "Last month's Cosmopolitan," she said, grinning.

"I'm buying you a lifetime subscription," he said breathlessly.

Ashley laughed out loud, nuzzling his neck, feeling extremely good, sated and ridiculously happy.

Sebastian gathered her closer to him, his lips against her forehead. Pulling back, he looked down at her. He waited until she looked up at him, his eyes stared directly into hers.

"I love you," he said, his tone both reverent and unwavering.

Ashley stared back at him, shocked into complete silence. She blinked a couple of times, sure that she must be dreaming.

"Sebastian..." she breathed, her look so awed that he couldn't mistake her feelings for him.

"I'm guessing you kind of like me too?" he said, his tone mild, his smile warm.

Ashley shook her head. "No, I'm basically madly in love with you," she said, her voice holding a note of humor.

"Well, that's handy," he said, grinning.

"Is it?" she asked, smiling at him.

"Oh yeah," he said, nodding as he pulled her closer to kiss her lips.

It was a nice way to wake up.

Later that morning, Sebastian pulled into the lot at the office and he saw Jet leaning against the open trunk of the Maserati. She was smoking and he could hear her music playing loudly. Getting out of his vehicle, he walked over to her.

"We set this morning, Mathews?" he asked, his tone formal. It was an indication of how distant things had been between them in the couple of weeks.

Jet's eyes narrowed as she blew out a stream of smoke and looked considering at her cigarette. "That's *Jet Fire* to you, Baz," she said, her tone wry.

Sebastian nodded, grinning, happy to hear it. Though his response was still a bit subdued.

"That so?" he asked.

Jet nodded, looking up at him. "Ash texted me," she said, her grin sly.

"I see," he said. "And I take it you approve?"

"Wholeheartedly," Jet said, smiling, as she extended her hand to him.

"Glad to hear it," he replied, his tone sincere as he clasped her hand in his. He then pulled her to him to hug her tight. "I'm sorry," he said, his tone tremulous.

"Me too," Jet said, closing her eyes for a moment.

They stayed that way for a full minute, then they moved apart, both of them nodding and grinning at the other.

"What'd I miss?" Skyler asked, her tone wry as she walked up, knowing full well the two had just finally made up.

"Not a damned thing," Sebastian said, grinning. "I'm gonna go make sure my team is ready to go, you girls headed over to the airport?"

"Yeah, change of plans," Skyler said. "We got a helo out of the LAPD Hooper Heliport."

"Why, what happened?" Jet asked.

"With Dev out of commission, we got no Air Force support," Skyler said. "So I'm borrowing one from LAPD, we're picking it up at the heliport. Jams is already over there doing the walk around."

Jet nodded, looking grim at the mention of Shenin.

"Wait," Sebastian said, "what's going on with Shenin?"

Jet and Skyler exchanged a look, few people knew at this point.

"Shenin tried to kill herself last night," Jet told him.

"Holy shi-..." Sebastian said, his look grim.

"Yeah," Jet said, nodding.

"Is she going to be okay?" he asked.

Jet nodded, looking at Skyler. "Yeah, she is," she said. Then to Skyler she asked, "You okay?"

Skyler shrugged slightly. "I'm dealing."

Sebastian gave Skyler a questioning look.

"Sky found her," Jet said, her tone gentle.

"In a pool of her own blood," Skyler added, looking sick.

Sebastian shook his head, blowing his breath out. He reached over and pulled Skyler into his arms, hugging her. Skyler accepted the hug with a smile; she knew it was how Sebastian lent his strength to people and she loved him for it.

"Alright," he said when he finally let Skyler go. "Let's do this."

An hour later, Jams and Skyler were flying in South West Los Angeles, over an area called Park Mesa Heights. It was a heavy Crips gang area in the city. They were following a suspect that Sebastian's team was hoping to finally connect to the money he was laundering for a Mexican Cartel.

"Come right ten degrees, Sky," Jet was saying, hearing the static feedback she'd been getting a lot. "Fuckin A!" she growled. "Sky, did you copy?" She waited, keyed the mic again and got a screech of feedback, yanking the helmet off her head she threw it across the cabin. Unbelting the straps, she got up, hearing a strange sound as she did.

"Sky!" Jet yelled, walking toward the cockpit.

Suddenly there was a screech of metal sheering off, and a loud snap. In the cockpit, Skyler suddenly had claxons blaring and lights going crazy.

"Fuck, fuck!" Skyler said. "What happened?" she yelled at Jams.

The helicopter began losing altitude and an alarming rate.

"Tail rotor is gone!" Jams yelled as both he and Skyler fought to control the decent of the aircraft.

"Jet hold on we're going down hard!" Skyler yelled, doing her best to keep the aircraft level, knowing their best chances were if they landed on the skids, at least in the initial impact.

Skyler and Jams fought the aircraft all the way down.

Sebastian saw that the helicopter was in trouble. He started calling it in, trying to discern the path. He had no idea what was happening, but he knew there was a problem; there was fire on the tail rotor.

"Eleven ninety-nine, officers down! Standby for location!" Sebastian yelled.

He tracked the helicopter visually, and started trying to figure out where Skyler was trying to put it down. There was a large parking lot at Crenshaw and West 60th, and that seemed to be the direction of the helicopter.

"Looks like they're headed for West sixtieth and Crenshaw, Saint John Evangelist Church parking lot! Send fire and rescue now!" he yelled.

He peeled off the surveillance, calling out a couple of his guys to follow him. Jamming on the accelerator he headed in that direction, constantly watching the helicopter get lower and lower.

"Damnit, damnit, damnit!" he was chanting as he drove.

He was two blocks away when he heard the helicopter's impact. He winced at the sound, praying he wasn't about to see a fireball erupt above the buildings. He skidded around another corner and saw the copter on its side; the tail section was on fire. He drove up into the lot, throwing his vehicle in park and jumping out to run to the crash.

Climbing on top of the helicopter, he tried to shove open the window, he could see that Skyler and Jams were both moving, unbuckling themselves.

"Cover!" Sebastian yelled to them, gesturing to the window.

Both Skyler and Jams covered their faces and put their heads down. Sebastian kicked the window with all the force he had, shoving it out of the frame.

"Come on!" he yelled, putting his hands down into the aircraft to reach for them. "Where's Jet?"

"In back! I can't get a response!" Skyler yelled, as she started to move to the cockpit doorway.

"No Sky! Get up here now! Jams grab her!"

Jams turned and grabbed Skyler, shoving her toward Sebastian's hands. Skyler fought him, not willing to leave Jet behind.

"Get up here, I'll get her!" Sebastian yelled.

Finally Skyler's hands were in his, and he pulled her out, then Jams followed. Sebastian dropped Skyler to the ground, she was coughing and bleeding from a cut on her forehead, but she seemed okay. Jams and Sebastian moved to the window. Sebastian looked inside, he couldn't see Jet, but smoke was starting to fill the back part of the cabin. Sebastian tried to kick out the window, but it only gave partially. The shatter proof glass splintered and only dropped out a few pieces, leaving a jagged small opening, not any of them could fit through.

"Jams get down there and be ready to take her," he told other man.

Sebastian grabbed ahold of either side of the glass and yanked as hard as he could, feeling the glass cut through his hands as he did. It took another two pulls, but finally the window gave and he was able to create an opening big enough for him to fit through. He got cut on the sides as he slid through, but ignored the burning sensation. His hands were bleeding, so he pulled off his shirt, ripping the sleeves to wrap them around his hands, even as he moved to locate Jet. She was lying on what had been the side of the cabin in a crumpled heap. She had no helmet on, her head was bleeding, and he could see she was unconscious.

"Jet!" he yelled, trying to get a response. Moving to kneel next to her, he checked for a pulse, he couldn't feel one. "Come on honey, give me a sign here..." he said, checking for her pulse again but he felt nothing. "Fuck!" he yelled. "Jams get the EMTs over here the minute they arrive, she's not breathing, I'm starting CPR!"

"You need to get the two of you out of there!" Jams yelled. "This thing is going to blow, get out of there now!"

Jams climbed back up on the side of the helicopter, and reached through the opening Sebastian had created. Sebastian picked Jet up as carefully as he could. Her body was completely lifeless; he could see blood coming from three different places, including her chest. He gritted his teeth and handed her up to Jams, just as he heard the ambulances arriving.

"Go!" he yelled at Jams, not wanting him to wait. They needed to get Jet medical attention immediately.

Jams jumped down and ran Jet's body over to the ambulance that had just stopped.

"Baz, get out of there!" Skyler yelled, moving to climb up on the helicopter.

The fire was moving closer to the fuel tank, and although they were designed not to blow up, gas and fire would always blow up.

"Get everybody back!" Sebastian yelled, as he jumped, grasping the side of the opening with his hand. He slipped because of the blood on his hands and landed back inside the helicopter with a loud thud.

"Fuck!" he yelled, moving to grab anything he could stand on to get closer to the opening. He found a chest, and stood on it, grasping the sides once again with his bleeding hands. He felt tingling and numbness in his hands and thought, *Nerve damage, just what I need.* This time he was able to pull himself up to leverage himself out of the helicopter.

He'd no sooner jumped down and moved Skyler back with him, than the helicopter exploded in a fireball. Regardless, they headed straight to the ambulance that Jams had taken Jet to and heard them doing CPR.

Sebastian and Skyler exchanged a look, both looking grave.

"Got a pulse!" one of the EMTs said. "Let's go!"

"Go, we'll be right behind you," Sebastian told Skyler.

Skyler didn't argue. She got into the back of the ambulance just as they started closing the doors. Sebastian and Jams watched the ambulance pull out, as the fire department pulled up to deal with the burning helicopter.

Less than an hour later, Fadiyah was walking through the doors to the hospital, feeling a complete sense of unreality. An officer had shown up at school, pulling her out of class and telling her that Jet had been injured in a crash and that she needed to come with him. She'd nodded, picking up her books and bag and following him numbly. Now walking through the hospital, the officer in the lead, she couldn't stop thinking that this wasn't happening. Jet couldn't be hurt, she'd just kissed her goodbye at school hours before, they must be wrong.

She saw Skyler and Sebastian standing in the waiting room with Kashena, Jericho and even Midnight Chevalier herself, having flown up from San Diego. Skyler saw Fadiyah first and walked straight over to the girl, taking her in her arms and hugging her.

"They have to be wrong," Fadiyah said, her tone faint. "Jet is not hurt, she cannot be…"

Skyler pulled back, looking down at the girl, she could see that she was in emotional shock at that point. Glancing at Sebastian, she nodded toward the chairs and moved Fadiyah toward them. Jericho, Kashena and Midnight all turned to watch Skyler sit Fadiyah down. Skyler knelt in front of the girl, taking Fadiyah's hands in hers, looking up into her eyes.

"Fadiyah," she said, her tone as gentle as she could make it. "When Sebastian found her in the copter, she had no pulse. The EMTs got her pulse back, but lost it twice on the way here… She's in surgery right now, but it doesn't look good… I need you to be prepared for the worst…"

Fadiyah blinked a couple of times, then she fell forward, fainting. Skyler caught her, and was almost thankful for the girl, it might make things easier for her if she wasn't awake for what might come. Sebastian stepped in, picking Fadiyah up and carrying her over to a couch, laying her down gently and looking over at Skyler. He was worried about Skyler as much as any of them. The way the helicopter had crashed was similar to the crash she'd been through in Iraq. He had no idea what this was doing to her emotionally. So far she'd been rock solid, he wasn't sure how long that was going to last. It lasted precisely ten more minutes, and then Devin walked in looking completely terrified.

"Sky!" she exclaimed, running to her wife, and throwing her arms around her. "Oh my God, all I was told was there was a crash and that you were all hurt, possibly killed…"

Skyler completely lost her composure then, and it took Sebastian, Devin and Jericho to move her to the chairs in the waiting room and calm her down.

"I killed her, I killed her," Skyler kept repeating, her hands shaking so badly that Sebastian motioned to Midnight to get a nurse.

In the end, they had to give Skyler a sedative. Even then, Skyler just sat and stared straight ahead, her thumb rubbing the palm of her other hand. Devin watched Skyler carefully, she knew that Skyler was right on the edge, and she knew she needed to watch her carefully.

At one point, Devin turned to Sebastian. "We don't leave her alone for a second right now."

He nodded, understanding exactly what she meant. They could be losing Jet as they sat there, and they'd already almost lost Shenin. They weren't going to take the chance of losing Skyler now too.

Slowly but surely the group showed up at the hospital. Quinn and Xandy walked over to Skyler and Devin. Xandy hugged Devin and Quinn talked quietly to Skyler. Skyler nodded a few times, closing her eyes slowly, then took Quinn's hand, squeezing it in thanks for her words. Cat and Jovina got there, they both hugged both women.

Quinn, who was sitting next to Skyler, nodded to both of them. Zoey arrived, hugging Jericho, then walked over to Skyler and Devin, talking softly to each of them, and hugging Skyler. Raine and Natalia arrived, moving to sit with the rest of the group, not wanting to intrude, but knowing they needed to be there.

Sierra rushed in at one point, hugging Kashena and Sebastian, being the first to really notice his hands and insisting that he get seen by a doctor. Sebastian was surprised to realize he'd forgotten about his hands completely. The blood had finally stopped, but the scraps of shirt were stuck to the wounds. While he was waiting for the doctor to come in, Ashley arrived, having finally been told when someone thought to call her.

"Sebastian..." Ashley said, walking into the exam room where Kashena had sent her. Then saw his hands. "Oh my God..." she said softly.

"I'm okay honey..." he said, his tone grave. "But Jet..."

Ashley looked at him, blinking a couple of times. "What?" she asked looking frightened.

"We're not sure if she's going to make it..." he said, knowing he was dealing her a blow and wishing like hell he didn't have to be the one to do it.

Ashley moved to sit in the chair next to where he sat on the exam table, all the color draining from her face. She shook her head, tears sliding down her cheeks. Sebastian moved to hold her, and she buried her head against his chest, crying in earnest. He held her doing everything he could to try to help, but they were all feeling the same pain.

It was hours until they were told anything. Jet's parents arrived from Seattle and immediately went to comfort Fadiyah, who'd finally come to, and sat stoically by herself. When Todd and Marcel arrived, however, she cried in Marcel's arms for over an hour.

When the doctor finally came out, Midnight directed him to the three sitting off to the side. He walked over to Marcel, Todd and Fadiyah, speaking directly to Jet's parents.

"Your daughter is in a very serious condition, she has a head injury, damage to one lung and a lot of internal bruising, so much that we can't even see clearly on the CT scan. We had her open for longer than we wanted to trying to repair the damage we could see. I have no idea what the next few hours will hold," he told them, his look sympathetic. "But I would prepare yourselves for the possibility that she won't regain consciousness and that she could very well die tonight."

Fadiyah closed her eyes, not wanting to hear what the doctor was saying, and sure that if she just shut her eyes she would find that this was all just a bad dream.

"Can we see her, doctor?" Marcel asked.

"Yes, right this way," the doctor said.

He led them to the recovery room Jet was in, she was hooked up to every machine imaginable, and there were bandages on her head, wrist and around her torso. Marcel and Todd walked over to their daughter, talking to her for a few minutes, leaning down and kissing her cheek, both crying as they did. They moved back then, giving Fadiyah the room to walk over to the side of the bed.

Fadiyah reached out with a hand that was shaking terribly, she touched Jet's cheek, her tears sliding down her face silently. She put her hand to Jet's forehead, leaning down to kiss her cheek and her lips softly. She put her hand in Jet's hand, lifting Jet's hand carefully, kissing the back of it, and putting Jet's palm to her cheek, crying harder as she did.

In the room the only sound was the beeping of monitors and Fadiyah's quiet sobs. Then they heard Jet groan softly. Fadiyah's head snapped up, her eyes focused on Jet's face. Jet was grimacing, her eyes still closed, but her breathing becoming labored. Fadiyah immediately pressed the button for the nurse, even as Todd strode out into the hallway.

Jet's eyes flew open, and she was gasping in pain, her eyes were on Fadiyah immediately.

"Jet!" Fadiyah said, holding Jet's hand and feeling Jet squeeze her hand repeatedly.

"Everything..." Jet said, her voice breathless, "Hurts... It hurts..." she said, tears in her eyes. She shook her head. "I'm sorry... honey... I'm sorry..." she said, her tone devastated. "I love you..." she said then, her breathing labored. She was writhing in pain.

"Jet! Hold on, please hold on," Fadiyah said, squeezing Jet's hand.

"Can't... hurts..." Jet said, her eyes pleading with Fadiyah. "Tell me you love me..." she said, haltingly.

"You know I do, Jet, but please, you have to hold on, you have to..." Fadiyah said, crying as she tried desperately to get through to Jet.

"Baby, please..." Jet said, her voice tearful and trembling. "Please tell me you love me... please..."

"I love you Jet, I love you," Fadiyah said, leaning down so her lips were right next to Jet's ear. "I love you, but you have to hold on, please…"

Jet shook her head, tears sliding from her eyes. "I can't honey… I'm so sorry…I love you…"

Fadiyah was holding Jet's hand and she literally felt the strength drain out of it as the monitor went to one long beep, signaling that Jet's heart had stopped.

Fadiyah let out a long keening wail and sank to her knees. Sebastian and Skyler had come running when they'd heard Todd tell the nurses that Jet was awake. They both just stared in shock. Skyler collapsed but fortunately Sebastian was still aware enough to catch her. Marcel cried in her husband's arms. Ashley, who'd followed Sebastian, leaned against the wall, crying silently.

The hospital staff responded instantly to the monitor and came on the run. Ashley had the presence of mind to go to Fadiyah, helping her up and getting her out of the way of the hospital staff who were trying to get Jet back. It was a nightmare scene, one none of them would ever forget.

Chapter 9

To everyone's shock and relief, the doctors and nurses managed to get Jet's pulse back. The doctors had gone back in surgically to find that Jet's spleen had ruptured, causing all the pain she was in when she woke. The pain had sent her body into shock, which had caused the cardiac arrest. After having surgery where the doctors were able to repair the rupture, Jet rested more comfortably. She was unconscious for two days.

When she woke, she looked up at the ceiling for a long time, and then slowly turned her head to see Fadiyah sitting in a chair next to her bed, asleep. Reaching out she gently touched Fadiyah's hand.

Fadiyah woke up instantly and smiled the most incredible smile Jet had ever seen.

"We have got to stop meeting like this," Jet said, her voice weak.

"Yes, that would be very good," Fadiyah replied, nodding. Then she leaned forward, her silver-gray eyes on Jet's. "We lost you, Jet," she said, her voice tremulous. "You died right in front of me…"

Jet closed her eyes slowly, then opened them again, looking up into Fadiyah's. "I'm sorry honey…" she said, saying the same words she had as she was dying. "I'm sorry."

Fadiyah shook her head. "You cannot ever do that again," she said, her tone so serious that Jet couldn't help but grin, which caused Fadiyah to narrow her eyes.

"I'll put that on the list of things I'm not allowed to do ever again," Jet responded, smiling softly.

"At the top of the list," Fadiyah said.

"You got it, babe," Jet said, grinning.

Todd and Marcel walked in at that moment.

"Jet…" Todd said, smiling at his daughter as he walked over to the side of the bed. Marcel moved to the other side, looking down at her daughter.

"You gave us a pretty good scare, young lady," Todd told Jet.

"So I hear," Jet said, her look serious.

"But you're better now, and that's what matters," Marcel said, reaching out to touch her daughter's cheek.

"She has promised me that she will never do that again," Fadiyah said, smiling over at Jet.

"Well, that's a good thing," Todd said, winking at Jet.

"Yes, it is," Marcel said, nodding.

"You guys look exhausted," Jet said. "Any chance I could get you two to take my girl home so you can all get some sleep?"

"Not likely," Todd said, looking over at Fadiyah. "Your girl has refused to move from your side for the last forty eight hours."

"Babe…" Jet said, looking over at Fadiyah.

Fadiyah folded her arms, looking at Jet. "My place is with you."

Marcel smiled. "How can you argue with that logic?"

"I can't," Jet said, smiling at Fadiyah. "But I can kick you two out of here," she said, looking at her parents. "Go, get some sleep, please."

Marcel and Todd looked at each other, nodding, knowing that it was taxing on Jet's strength to have too many people around her anyway.

"You win," Todd said, smiling and leaning down to kiss his daughter's cheek. "But we'll be back tomorrow."

"We will see you both tomorrow, honey," Marcel said, leaning down to kiss Jet.

They both kissed Fadiyah's forehead before they left. Jet watched, seeing the smile on Fadiyah's face.

"Oh, look who's back in the land of the living," Sebastian said, as he walked into the room with Ashley right behind him.

"Jet!" Ashley cried, rushing over to lean down and hug Jet carefully.

"Hi Ash…" Jet said, smiling. Then she heard Ashley sniffle. "And stop that right now," she said, narrowing her eyes.

"Sorry," Ashley said, wiping at her tears, even as she smiled.

Jet held her hand up to Sebastian then saw the bandages on his hands.

"What happened?" Jet asked.

"How about we worry about you for a minute, Jet Fire," Sebastian said, leaning down to kiss her cheek. "You scared the shit out of me," he said, looking down into her eyes.

"Not on purpose," Jet said smiling.

"Don't care," he said. "Don't do it again."

"Sir, yes sir," Jet said, grinning.

"You used up a few of your lives on this one, young lady," he told her.

"Well, I know at least one," she said, looking over at Fadiyah.

"Try four," he said, his look serious.

"Eesh," Jet said, looking surprised. "How are Sky and Jams?" she asked then.

"They weren't badly hurt in the crash," Sebastian said. "Sky's been a wreck though."

Jet drew in a deep breath, blowing it out and nodding. "It wasn't her fault, though, she knows that right?"

Sebastian gave her a perplexed look. "They're still investigating the cause," he said. "Why, what do you know?"

"There was a sound like a rattling, before all hell broke loose, and then a screech of metal, like something sheering off… That helicopter was fucked up, Baz, the comms didn't even work."

Sebastian looked contemplative, then nodded. "I'll get them looking in that direction, Midnight wants answers, and she's going to get them. But I tend to wonder if she was going to get the right ones… This will help, Jet Fire, good job," he said, winking at her.

Jet looked at Fadiyah. "I need to see Sky," she told her.

Fadiyah nodded, getting up and leaving the room to get Skyler. Ashley and Sebastian left when Skyler entered the room. Sebastian leaned over and kissed Skyler on the forehead as he passed her. Fadiyah also left them alone.

Skyler walked over to the bed, looking down at Jet, her look dazed.

"Sky," Jet said, holding up her hand.

Skyler looked at Jet's hand, and then took it, moving to sit down next to the bed. "Jet, I'm so sorry…" Skyler began.

"No," Jet said, shaking her head. "You have nothing to be sorry for, that helicopter was fucked up, Sky."

"What?" Skyler asked.

"Something broke," Jet said. "I don't know what the hell it was, but something sheared off right before the helicopter went nuts, they need to figure out what happened. You know the comms were all fucked up, and there was a sound like a rattling before I got up to come tell you about it. That's when there was that shriek of metal and then everything went to shit…"

Skyler looked at her for a long moment, her thoughts obviously racing. "The controls went cold…" she said. "Jams said we lost our rotor… If the vertical stabilizer ripped… Took out the rotor…" She was muttering to herself and Jet could see that she was coming out of her fog.

"Got some thinking to do, huh?" Jet asked.

Skyler looked at her, shaking her head. "You may have just saved my career," She said, smiling and feeling a bit like a weight had lifted off her.

"Anytime," Jet said.

Skyler gave her a serious look then. "We watched you die," she said, her tone grave, the look in her eyes devastated.

"Believe me, it was never the plan," Jet told her. "And if it makes you feel any better, I've been told that I'm not allowed to do it again, ever," she said, with a grin.

Skyler looked back at her. "I have never seen someone as devastated by a loss as Fadiyah was, you could hear that wail throughout the hospital."

Jet's look flickered. "I heard it," she said, a bit bewildered. "I don't know how, but I heard it… And I'll never forget it."

"Don't," Skyler said, "because that my friend was true devotion."

Jet nodded, looking affected.

"You need to get some sleep," Jet said, getting tired again herself. She reached out for Skyler's hand, and squeezed it gently. "Please take care of yourself, Sky. And stop blaming yourself, it was not your fault."

Skyler nodded, starting to look like she believed it.

Getting up, she leaned over to kiss Jet on the head. "Don't fuckin' scare me like that again," she said, her eyes staring down into Jet's.

"Roger that," Jet said, grinning.

Skyler left then and Fadiyah came back in. Jet was already getting tired, so Fadiyah simply sat, stroking her hand until she fell asleep.

Jet woke an hour later. She was lying on her side looking at Fadiyah. The girl was curled up in an uncomfortable looking chair, trying to sleep and very obviously failing.

"Fadi," Jet said, reaching her hand out to touch Fadiyah's leg.

"Hmmm?' Fadiyah murmured tiredly.

"Honey, you can't sleep that way," Jet said.

"I can," Fadiyah said, getting a stubborn tone in her voice.

"Baby, come here," Jet said, holding out her right arm.

"What?" Fadiyah asked softly, not understanding what Jet wanted.

"Come *here*, babe…" Jet said, touching the bed next to her.

"But…" Fadiyah said, shaking her head.

"Come here, or I'm coming over there," Jet said, grinning at the implausibility of her own statement, but it was enough to convince Fadiyah.

Fadiyah climbed carefully into the bed with Jet, careful to avoid the wires to the monitors and rested her head in the hollow of Jet's shoulder, sighing as she did. Jet carefully put her arms around Fadiyah, feeling better herself. Moments later they were both asleep.

Later during the night the nurse came to take Jet's vital signs, she was surprised to find the dark haired girl in bed with her patient. Jenny, the nurse, like many others in the hospital that evening had been on duty the night Jet Mathews had 'died' and the dark haired girl had wailed eerily. Jenny was very happy to see that Jet had not only been spared, but seemed to be doing well now. As Jenny checked Jet's pulse, with her hand on Jet's wrist, she looked over to see that Jet's eyes were open tiredly. Jenny smiled at Jet, who smiled tiredly in response, then closed her eyes again and was asleep immediately. In all her life, Jenny wished for a love like these two obviously had.

Across town Sebastian and Ashley were lying in bed, her head on his chest, his eyes staring up at the ceiling as he absently stroked her shoulder.

Ashley turned to look up at him. "I heard what you did the day of the crash."

Sebastian looked down at her, his look somber.

"Climbing into a helicopter that's on fire," Ashley said, her look concerned. "That's pretty brave, Sebastian."

"Brave or crazy?" he asked her.

"A little, or maybe a lot, of both," she said.

He nodded. "You know I had to," he told her.

Ashley nodded. "I know, it's who you are."

He nodded again. "I couldn't leave her in there."

"I'm glad you didn't," she said. "As much for her, as for you."

"For me?" he asked, surprised by her statement.

"You'd never have forgiven yourself, Sebastian."

He looked back at her for a long moment, and then nodded. "You're right about that."

"I know," she said, smiling. "And I love that about you."

"Might have loved me a little less if I hadn't gotten out in time…" He said.

"Well, you would have been a little harder to love, since you'd have been dead," she said, her words sounding like she was joking, but her eyes belying those words.

"Well, I'm not."

"No, you're not."

His hand reached up to touch her cheek, bandages still in place. "I love you."

She moved to kiss his lips, then kissed each of his hands. "I love you."

They were both silent for a few minutes, Ashley's fingers touched the bandages on his hands gently.

"Are your hands going to be okay?" she asked him.

Sebastian shrugged slightly. "The doctor said that there's a surgeon who can fix any damage, but he's expensive. Jet's dad said he'd pay for whatever I needed .. Not sure how I feel about that."

Ashley moved to lever herself up on her elbows to look down at him. "If you don't, Jet'll just do it," she told him, knowing Jet owed Sebastian her life.

Sebastian pursed his lips. "Figured as much, yeah."

"Dangerous stuff, saving people's lives," Ashley said, grinning. "They tend to be grateful."

"Damnit," he said, winking at her.

"Oh, I almost forgot!" Ashley said suddenly.

"What?" Sebastian asked.

"Juliet is coming for a visit next week," Ashley told him.

"Uh," he stammered, surprised.

"I told her about the accident and all and she wants to come see you," Ashley told him.

Sebastian grimaced. "God…" he said, sounding like the classic big brother.

"Sebastian, she loves you and she wants to make sure you're okay." He blew his breath out in consternation, but nodded all the same.

***

For two days, Tyler had not left Shenin's bedside in the hospital, not to eat, not to sleep; only for the very basic needs, and then she was straight back in the chair watching her wife. Skyler had come in to see Shenin the evening they'd gotten to the hospital. Tyler had hugged Skyler, thanking her over and over for saving Shenin's life. She knew that if Skyler had not gone to the apartment and found Shenin when she did, Shenin would not be alive. Skyler had been deeply affected by the event and it had taken both Devin and Jet to talk her down. Muffit had been cleaned and was now, much to the hospital administrator's horror, lying right next to Shenin on the hospital bed. She would frequently put her paw on Tyler's hand that was clasped in Shenin's, and move to lick Tyler's face as well.

When Shenin finally opened her eyes, Tyler was there, her bright blue eyes were the first thing Shenin saw.

"There's my girl…" Tyler said, smiling down at Shenin.

"Ty…" Shenin whispered.

"Right here, honey… right here," Tyler said, squeezing her hand gently.

Shenin nodded, closing her eyes slowly, then opening them again and looking at Tyler. "I heard you…" she said, her voice soft.

"I love you," Tyler said, leaning down to kiss Shenin's lips softly. "As long as I have you, I have everything I'll ever need."

Shenin's eyes filled with tears then, spilling over as she closed her eyes. "I'm so sorry, Ty…" she said, her voice mournful.

"You're still here, baby, you're still with me," Tyler said, tears in her own eyes. "That's all the matters."

Shenin nodded, closing her eyes again.

There had been a note found in Shenin's bedroom at the apartment. It read:

"I'm sorry I wasn't able to tell you everything... I couldn't hurt you like that... I'm sorry I'm not strong enough to withstand this pain... I love you, Tyler, I will always love you."

Tyler had been physically sick upon reading it. She'd crumbled it up and thrown it away.

She was never going to let her wife feel this low again. She didn't care what it took.

***

The night Shenin was released from the hospital, she lay in bed, watching her wife move around the room as she got ready for bed. She was still feeling very shell-shocked by everything that had happened. They'd heard about Jet the day before, and Tyler had gone over to that wing of the hospital to check in on her, even if it was only for an update. Shenin had been released only that afternoon, as she'd been on a seventy-two hour hold for a suicide watch. Only fast talking and some help from other sources had kept Shenin out of the psych ward.

Tyler moved to the bed, getting in and laying down, pulling Shenin into her arms immediately.

"Jet's okay?" Shenin asked, not for the first time that night.

"Yes, honey, she's okay," Tyler confirmed.

Shenin nodded, looking pensive. Tyler reached up to stroke Shenin's cheek with her hand, pressing her lips to Shenin's forehead. They lay quietly for a few minutes, then Shenin looked up at Tyler.

"Ty..." she began, her eyes looking haunted. "I know... that there's a lot of things I need to tell you..." she said, her voice hesitant.

"About Iraq?" Tyler asked gently.

Shenin's eyes reflected surprise, but she nodded slowly.

"You don't have to tell me, Shen," Tyler said, her look searching. "Jet told me, everything."

Shenin's eyes widened in surprise, then took on an angry look.

"Babe, don't get mad at her, I kind of forced her hand," Tyler said, grimacing.

"What did you do?" Shenin asked, looking worried.

"I kinda punched her."

"Oh my God, Ty..." Shenin breathed.

"Yeah, I know, it was stupid," Tyler said. "But I was desperate at that point."

Shenin nodded her head, understanding what Tyler meant. Things had gone really sideways at that point and there didn't seem to be any way to stop it from happening. When she had awoken from the nightmare, she'd seen Tyler as the man who'd raped her repeatedly, and all she'd wanted to do was to get away. Even when Tyler had told her it was her, Shenin's mind wouldn't accept it and she kept fighting to get away. In her mind if she just fought a little bit harder, he wouldn't have succeeded, and wouldn't have killed her marriage. It had been that thought that had led to the punch to Tyler's face. It had been that punch and Tyler's walking out that had led to her actions on the kitchen floor.

"I'm so sorry, Ty..." Shenin said, her voice breaking as tears slid down her face.

She shook her head, knowing that there was nothing she could do now to erase what she'd done, that nothing was going to take that memory away for Tyler.

"Can you tell me what was going through your mind?" Tyler asked, her voice gentle.

Shenin drew in a deep breath, her eyes unfocused as she carefully worked her way around the memory.

"When I hit you, and you left…" Shenin said, looking up at Tyler. "I thought to myself, that I had just done it… finished it… I was done…" she said, her voice trailing off as Tyler pulled her in close, doing her best not to blame herself for everything. "I just thought it would be easier for everyone if I wasn't here anymore. You could move on with your life, find someone that wasn't so fucked up…"

"Oh babe…" Tyler said, tears in her eyes now. "No…" she said, shaking her head. "I can't live without you, Shenin. I'm not saying that for effect, I mean every word. If I had lost you… I don't think I would have hung on for long," she said, her tone tremulous. "You are my life, Shen, and if you aren't here, I don't want to be here either."

Shenin looked back at Tyler, surprised by what she was saying.

"But Ty… your family, your parents…" she said, thinking about all the people who would be affected by Tyler's death.

"Shenin," Tyler said, her hand on Shenin's chin, tilting her face up to hers. "You are all that matters to me. If I have you, I have everything I need."

Shenin looked back at her wife for a long moment, trying to take in what Tyler was saying. No one had ever valued her on this level before, and she found it hard to believe anyone could.

Tyler could see that Shenin was struggling with what she was hearing. Part of Tyler knew that Shenin was never going to believe everything she was saying, but it was Tyler's hope that if Shenin at least took some of it in, it would help heal the some of the wounds that had allowed her to take such drastic steps to end her pain.

Holding Shenin's face in her hands, Tyler looked down into her eyes. "I need to apologize to you," she said, her voice gentle, but strong.

"Ty…" Shenin said, starting to shake her head.

"Shen, please let me finish," Tyler whispered.

Shenin bit her lip, nodding, her eyes reflecting worry about what Tyler was trying to apologize for.

"No, I'm not apologizing for Iraq," Tyler said, knowing it was exactly what Shenin was thinking. The look on Shenin's face then, proved she was right. "I know there was no way I could have been there, or could have known what would happen, so it's something that I need to put aside. What I am going to stop putting aside," she said, looking more intent, "is you."

"What?" Shenin asked, looking confused.

"Babe, I've let the fucking Air Force change my priorities, and now I'm changing them back. You," she said, her look pointed, "are my priority and if the Air Force doesn't like it, the Air Force is down a soldier."

"But Ty—"

"No, Shen," Tyler said, shaking her head, "there have been too many buts… I want to be here with you, but… I needed to be in Iraq with you, but… No, no more. I'm done. If they want to keep me they will transfer me to El Segundo, or I'm done. I will resign my commission. You are my priority Shenin, you need me, and I'm going to be here for you, no matter what that means."

Shenin drew in a deep breath, nodding her head.

"I love you…" Tyler said, leaning down to kiss Shenin's lips.

"I love you, Ty…" Shenin said, her hand at Tyler's waist, curled around a handful of Tyler's shirt.

"Now, there is something I am going to require of you," Tyler said, her look serious.

"What?" Shenin asked.

"No more messing around with this depression stuff. I need to know that you're gonna be okay when things get rough, and they will get rough babe, life just does that… I seriously want to look into medication and therapy, okay?"

Shenin swallowed convulsively, and then nodded. "Okay."

"Good," Tyler said, having been worried that Shenin wouldn't want to think about that kind of thing. "We will get through this babe… I promise you that. I will be with you every single step of the way, but you're going to have to take those steps, okay?"

"I know," Shenin said, nodding. "As long as you're with me, I can try."

"That's all I'm asking for, honey," Tyler said.

***

In Malibu, Devin lay holding Skyler against her. They were both feeling relieved over the discovery that the helicopter had indeed been brought down due to mechanical failure and through no fault of Skyler or Jams. The helicopter's vertical stabilizer had sheared off mid-flight and had caused the rotor blade and gearbox to separate from the tail section. Once again, Skyler was commended for her piloting skills, managing to bring the helicopter down on its skids, before it rolled, keeping them all from being killed on impact. The investigation determined that the only reason Jet had been hurt as severely as she had was because she hadn't been buckled in at the time of the crash.

"Are you okay?" Devin asked, stroking Skyler's hair.

Skyler blew her breath out, nodding her head.

"I mean, really okay, Sky," Devin said, her tone strong.

Skyler pulled back, looking at Devin, her light blue-green eyes staring directly into her wife's eyes. "Yes, babe, I am. Thinking that I'd done something wrong, that I almost got Jet killed… that was what messed me up."

"I know," Devin said. "I just need to know that you believe what that investigation is saying, and that you're still not harboring some kind of guilt over this."

Skyler shook her head. "No, I'm not," she said. "What Jet said, made sense, I just didn't know any of that at the time. All I knew was that we suddenly lost control. You start thinking of all the things that could have gone wrong, and it always comes back down to the pilot. Pilot error is the one thing you don't want to hear when someone you love was almost killed."

Devin nodded. "I understand that," she said, her voice soft.

Skyler nodded, taking another deep breath and blowing it out.

She looked at Devin then. "I'm sorry if I scared you," she said, knowing that her own PTSD had been amplifying her reactions to the situation.

She'd relived the crash of her Blackhawk years before over and over in her head, and had actually started to convince herself that crash had been her fault too. She'd started to think she was cursed and that she should never fly again... It had been a dangerous rabbit hole to go down. But Devin had been there by her side the entire time, holding on to her tight. She'd felt it, even in her darkest place.

"Thank you," Skyler said, her voice solemn.

"For what, Sky?" Devin asked.

Skyler smiled softly. "For being here, for going through this with me... for just... being you."

Devin smiled, tears misting her eyes. "I'm just glad you let me in this time."

"And I will try to always let you in," Skyler said.

"Good," Devin said, relieved beyond words.

***

Jet was finally released from the hospital a week after the crash. It drove her crazy, but she was required to rest once home as well. Fadiyah was insistent. Jet's parents also stayed to make sure that Fadiyah had all the help she needed with their hardheaded daughter.

Jet was sitting up in bed, watching whatever random things were on TV when her father walked into the room.

"We have a problem," he said, handing Jet an envelope.

It was an official looking envelope with an equally official letter inside telling Fadiyah that her student visa was being revoked due to lack of completion of her courses. The letter went on to say that Fadiyah would be deported in no more than thirty days.

"Well, fuck…" Jet said, looking at her dad.

An hour later, Fadiyah walked into their bedroom and saw that Jet was deep in thought.

"What is wrong?" Fadiyah asked immediately.

Jet looked at her, then touched the bed next to her. "Come here, we need to talk," Jet said, her tone serious.

Fadiyah hesitated, worried that something had come up with Jet's health, a test that came back or a new concern. She moved to sit in front of Jet on the bed, her eyes searching Jet's face, trying to discern the new danger.

Jet handed Fadiyah the letter from the embassy. Fadiyah read it, then looked at Jet, looking shocked and already scared.

"What can I do?" Fadiyah asked, her voice trembling.

Jet drew in a deep breath, shrugging slightly. "I've got a solution, but you're going to need to do something first," she said.

"What do I need to do? I will do whatever I need to, I cannot leave you…" Fadiyah said, her tone worried.

Again, Jet blew her breath out. "Well, your part is pretty easy," she said.

"Okay…" Fadiyah said, her voice trailing off as she tried to figure out why Jet looked so resolved.

"You need to say yes," Jet said simply.

Fadiyah looked mystified. "To what?" she asked, thinking in terms of some kind of oath.

"To a question," Jet said, her look direct.

"What is the question?" Fadiyah asked.

Jet tilted her head, her look thoughtful. "Whether or not you'll marry me," she said, her tone so casual that Fadiyah wasn't sure she'd heard her correctly.

"I am sorry?" Fadiyah said, blinking a couple of times.

Jet grinned. "Fadiyah Antar, will you marry me?"

Fadiyah's mouth dropped open, then she began nodding. "I would love to marry you!" she said, throwing her arms around Jet's neck.

Jet laughed, hugging her happily.

Fadiyah pulled back then, her look hesitant. "But if this is for me to stay in America..."

"Are you asking me if that's the only reason I'm asking you?" Jet queried.

Fadiyah nodded her head, afraid to say the words.

"No, babe," Jet said sincerely. "No, I knew when I woke up in that hospital room and I wasn't dead, that you were the reason I stayed. I need to honor that."

Fadiyah lay her hand on Jet's cheek, her silver-gray eyes staring back into Jet's. "I would be honored to be your wife."

"Good, 'cause we're gonna need to do, at the very least, a court ceremony quick," Jet said, grinning. "But we can plan something more… formal later. Okay?"

"Formal?" Fadiyah asked.

"Yeah, you know, if you want something big like Sky and Devin's, or whatever," Jet said, smiling. "Anything you want babe, however you want it."

"Anything?" Fadiyah queried, looking quizzical.

"Yes, anything," Jet confirmed, her light green eyes shining. "If you want it to be completely American, or you want to do a traditional Shia ceremony, or somewhere in between, I'm in, okay?"

Fadiyah smiled, tears in her eyes. It was no wonder she loved this woman so much.

There was a party held at their house a week later, ostensibly to celebrate Jet's recovery. At one point, during the party, Jet got everyone's attention.

"So, we're having this party, but we need to invite you all to another one in two weeks," Jet said, grinning.

"Is this going to become a habit?" Skyler asked, grinning at her friend.

"Nah," Jet said, "just trying to keep up." She winked at Skyler. "This next party will be held at 12400 Imperial Highway in Norwalk."

Everyone looked mystified, looking at each other to see if anyone else knew what that address was.

"I can see you all don't know what's located there," Jet said, "so let me help you out. That would be the County Recorder's Office, where they hand out marriage licenses…"

"Oh my God!" Skyler exclaimed, as everyone else gave varied shouts of shock and disbelief.

Skyler moved to hug Jet and in turn Fadiyah, as did everyone else.

"I don't see a ring…" Sebastian said, his tone sly.

"You will," Jet said mischievously.

Fadiyah glanced at Jet, but said nothing, surprised by her comment.

***

The weekend following the party, the group met up at their usual Saturday morning place of the gym. As always, the femme girls did Natalia's cardio dance class, and the butch girls did mixed martial arts training or just used weights. Usually by the time Natalia's class was winding down, all of the butches were there watching their respective girls dance. Sebastian had been included with the group since he and Kashena had arrived in LA, but now he was there to watch Ashley. His sister Juliet had also wanted to try Natalia's class since she was there visiting. Ashley and Juliet had become fast friends.

Everyone in the group was now fully aware that Sebastian was in love with Ashley, and they all fully approved of the match. Kashena was thrilled to see Sebastian so happy and was grateful to Ashley for that. Sebastian had just walked back over to the half wall that many of the girls were standing at, looking for Ashley. He overheard Kashena, Quinn, and Skyler discussing one of the women in the class.

"She's definitely butch…" Skyler said.

"I dunno, she's got some pretty good rhythm and moves," Kashena pointed out.

"Hey, we butches aren't friggin' robots," Quinn said, grinning.

"What's goin' on here?" Sebastian asked, moving to stand next to the three.

"Oh, the usual," Kashena said, grinning. "Checking out the new people and the endless game of is she or isn't she…"

"Seriously?" he asked. "You bois have nothing better to discuss?"

"Bite me," Kashena said, grinning. "It's kind of a sport."

Sebastian shook his head. "Okay, so who are we discussing?"

"The blond next to your girl, actually," Skyler said.

Sebastian looked over, seeing the girl with the bleach blond hair that Skyler was referring to. She was on the skinny side, but the tank top and shorts she wore exposed a great deal of lean muscle. She definitely had a butch look to her. She also looked very young.

"Looks like a swimmer, maybe," Sebastian said. "A lot of lean muscle, not bulky at all."

The women looked back over at the girl, nodding as they agreed with what Sebastian was saying.

"What's your gaydar say?" Kashena asked Sebastian.

"Oh yeah, definitely family," Sebastian said, grinning.

"Baz's gaydar is usually better than mine," Kashena told the other two.

"Who?" Jericho asked as she and Jet walked up.

The class was down to the last song where they were doing stretching. Ashley was breathing heavily, feeling like she probably overdid it, but she always enjoyed the class and she knew she needed to stay in good shape to keep up with Sebastian. She grinned at Juliet, Sebastian's sister, who was rolling her eyes and shaking her head; she'd had a rough time keeping up too.

Suddenly Ashley felt a wave of dizziness hit her. She figured it was because she'd just leaned over to stretch, so she moved to straighten up. Her vision went dark then.

"Baz..." Kashena said, as she saw Ashley start to fall.

Fortunately, the girl they'd just been discussing saw Ashley's movement and turned in time to put her body in the way of Ashley falling to the floor. Holding Ashley's arms, she carefully lowered her to the ground. Sebastian ran over, going down to his knees to reach for Ashley, and Juliet moved to Ashley as well. Sebastian moved to support Ashley, taking her from the blond haired girl.

"Thank you," he told the girl.

"No problem," the girl said, moving to stand.

Jet walked up, looking at the girl and recognizing her.

"Cody?" Jet queried.

"Jet, hey," Cody replied, nodding to her.

"Is she okay, Baz?" Jet asked.

Ashley was already coming to, looking around bewildered.

"What happened?" she asked.

"You passed out," Sebastian said.

"Oh, crap," Ashley said, grinning.

"Another Natalia victim," Quinn said, grinning.

"Hey, hey!" Natalia exclaimed, walking up to the group. "Callete juera!" she said, winking at Quinn. "This was not my fault."

"Think you can stand?" Sebastian asked Ashley.

"Yeah," Ashley said.

Sebastian helped her up.

"I'll take her to the bathroom, make sure she's okay," Jet said, moving to Ashley's arm to escort her away from the group, sensing that Ashley was extremely embarrassed.

Sebastian looked at the girl who Jet had referred to as Cody, extending his hand to her.

"Again, thank you," he said. "Sebastian Bach, that's my girlfriend Ashley."

Cody nodded, her hazel eyes sparkling. "Cody Falco," she said.

"Well, you saved the day, Cody," Jericho said, nodding at the girl, thinking she looked familiar. "Where do you work?" she asked.

"LAPD, TRACE task force," Cody said, recognizing Jericho Tehrani, the Director of the Division of Law Enforcement for the DOJ.

Jericho nodded. "That's where I recognize you from."

Cody nodded and then glanced at the clock. "Well, nice meeting you all, but I gotta go," she said, moving to pick up her gym bag. She put her hand up in a kind of salute wave.

The group watched the girl leave, seeing her take out a helmet and climb onto a black Ninja in the lot and riding away.

"Alrighty then," Sebastian said, grinning.

In the bathroom, Jet leaned against the wall, looking at Ashley who was putting cool water on her face. Glancing at Jet, she grinned.

"What?" Ashley asked.

Jet narrowed her eyes, her lips pursed. "Does he know?" she asked.

"What are you talking about?" Ashley asked.

Jet canted her head. "Do you even know?"

"What?" Ashley asked, looking at her strangely.

"Ash…" Jet said. "You got sick at the house twice the other day, you said your stomach has been bothering you… Now you're fainting…"

Ashley's mouth dropped open, but then she closed it shaking her head. "No, it's probably just flu."

Jet drew her breath in. "Might want to check, is all I'm saying…"

Later that night Sebastian was lying in bed, partially sitting up, his elbow bent, his head resting on his fist when Ashley walked into the bedroom.

Sebastian looked up at her, and caught the caution in her eyes.

"What's up?" he asked her.

Ashley moved to sit down, her look serious. Sebastian sat up, looking worried.

"What is it, Ash?" he asked.

"Sebastian," Ashley said, her tone solemn. She took a deep breath, knowing she needed to get it out. "I'm pregnant."

Surprise flickered across his face, but also relief and he let his breath out slowly.

"Okay…" he said, his tone guarded.

"I'm on the pill. But… I don't know it happened," she said plaintively.

He nodded. Ashley couldn't read the look on his face.

"I know this is a lot. And I know that you and I are… well, I mean…" she said, finally letting her voice trail off as she realized she had no idea what to say.

His look was contemplative. "I need to know what you want to do," he said, his tone even.

Ashley looked back at him; she hadn't really thought about that part. She'd been so freaked out by the idea that she was pregnant that she hadn't thought past having to tell him.

"I don't know," she told him honestly.

Sebastian nodded looking serious. "Would you consider marrying me and keeping it?" he asked, his voice subdued.

Ashley looked back at him, blinking. "Would I consider it?" she asked, her tone incredulous.

"Yeah," Sebastian said looking a bit unsure. "I don't want to lose you, or our baby," he said then.

Ashley shook her head looking at him with disbelief. "You think I want to leave you and take this baby away?"

"I don't know," he said, his look almost fearful.

"Oh my God, Sebastian," Ashley said, shaking her head. "No, I don't want to be anywhere but right here with you, and of course I'll marry you, I love you."

He smiled then, pulling her into his arms, and kissing her deeply. "Then I guess Jet's not the only one getting married, is she?"

"No, I guess not," Ashley said, with a smile of her own.

***

A week later, Jet woke Fadiyah with a kiss and then handed her a small box. Fadiyah moved to sit up, looking at Jet and then at the box.

"Open it," Jet told her.

Fadiyah opened the box and nestled inside black velvet was the most incredible ring Fadiyah had ever seen in her life. The center stone was a rectangular radiant cut red topaz, surrounded by small round cut stones in various colors ranging from orange to red and even a spring green. The band of the ring was lined with rectangular diamonds that winked and sparkled in the morning sunlight.

"Oh Jet…" Fadiyah said, unable to even think of words to explain how beautiful she thought the ring was.

For Jet, Fadiyah's face said it all. "You needed something as exquisite and unique as you are," she told Fadiyah, touching her face, smiling at her.

"I love it," Fadiyah said. "But…" she said, looking worried.

"Don't even ask about the money," Jet said with a beatific smile.

Considering the ring was made by designer Martin Katz, and topped out at eighteen carats for all the stones, the ring had cost a small fortune, but the way Jet saw it, it was for the rest of their lives.

Fadiyah bit her lip unable to fathom how much the ring had cost Jet, but also knowing Jet was never likely to tell her. She was able to gauge easily by people's reaction to it later that day.

"Holy shit!" Sebastian said, glowering at ring, and looking at Jet. "You do not disappoint, Jet Fire, I will give you that."

Jet grinned.

"Wow…" Kashena said, looking at the ring, then grinning at Jet. "Ya did good," she said.

Other comments were, "Hope it's insured," from Quinn, and "Cho! Co!" from Skyler. It was a Cajun expression for "Wow!" that caused Fadiyah to look confused and Jet to grin.

The civil ceremony proceeded easily enough, and then everyone went into the city to Morton's Steakhouse in Beverly Hills. Jet had reserved a private room. There were bottles of champagne, wine and outrageously expensive steaks. Everyone had a great time.

At one point, Sebastian announced to the group that he and Ashley were not only getting married, but expecting a child. That announcement threw the party into a whole new level, with everyone congratulating the couple. Jet bought Sebastian a thousand dollar bottle of champagne, apologizing to Ashley that she couldn't drink any. In the end, Jet, Kashena and Skyler helped him drink it.

"So…" Kashena said to Sebastian, as the party was winding down. "Didn't even tell me first, huh?" she asked.

Sebastian grinned. "We wanted to announce it, Kash." She nodded, clapping him on the shoulder. "Congratulations partner," she said to him, truly happy for him. "It's gonna be a beautiful kid, God help you if it's a girl…"

"Bite your tongue…" Sebastian said, scowling at her.

Kashena laughed, shaking her head.

Later, on a private plane, Jet looked over at Fadiyah. "You okay?" she asked. Fadiyah had seemed quite awestruck most of the day.

Fadiyah nodded. "I am just trying to take everything in, Jet," she said. "This has been such an amazing day."

"I'm glad," Jet said smiling. "Mrs. Mathews," she added.

Fadiyah's eyes widened, then she bit her lip. "That is my name now," she said, sounding awestruck.

"Yep," Jet said, nodding.

"I am so very lucky, Jet…" Fadiyah said.

"You and me both, babe, you and me both," Jet replied, kissing her deeply as the plane took off for Seattle, the one place Fadiyah wanted to go for their mini-honeymoon.

Jet had been surprised, but willing to do whatever Fadiyah wanted.

***

Shenin and Tyler had gone to their first counseling session, and it had been a rough one. The counselor had Shenin talk about the way she felt at that moment, and the way she wanted to feel going forward.

Afterwards, Tyler had taken Shenin to look at the apartment she wanted to rent them. They'd already talked about selling the house in Maryland. Tyler's threat had paid off and she was officially transferred to Los Angeles Air Force Base. The Air Force hadn't been willing to lose Captain Tyler Hancock as an asset. Tyler wanted to sell the house in Maryland and planned to buy one in Los Angeles, telling Shenin that their life was in Los Angeles now. Shenin happily went along with whatever Tyler wanted, just happy that they were weathering the storm that had threatened to destroy them.

That night, as they lay in bed, Tyler looked down at Shenin.

"Can you share anything about Iraq with me?" she asked gently.

Shenin looked up at her, knowing that Tyler was just trying to understand and help her through everything. She nodded slowly, looking contemplative.

"I remember the smell," she said. "Like dirt and sweat." She swallowed convulsively. "I had your riding kerchief and I remember just holding it to my nose and trying to breathe you in…" Her voice trailed off as she saw tears spring to Tyler's eyes.

She reached up, touching Tyler's cheek, her own eyes glazed with tears.

"I knew that I couldn't tell you what happened, I knew it would hurt you too much… I tried to pretend it wasn't happening and I just kept my thoughts on you. Even then, Ty, you were the reason I survived," she said, her voice a soft whisper.

"Going forward," Tyler said, after a few long moments. "What are you afraid of?" Shenin drew in a breath again, blowing it out slowly. "I don't know if I can have kids, Ty..." she said, her voice trembling. "I don't know if my body will handle it."

Tyler nodded. "Well, we can get that checked out," she said.

For a couple of years they'd discussed at length that Shenin was going to be the one to carry a baby. They'd had tests and had found that Tyler was really not designed for having babies. The doctors had warned that Tyler would have a really rough time in labor and Shenin hadn't been willing to take that chance. She still wasn't.

"If you can't, we can adopt if you want to," Tyler said. "It's not important," she said, shaking her head. "You being healthy and us being together is what's important."

Shenin nodded, knowing that Tyler meant mentally healthy.

"And all the rest?" Shenin asked, wondering if she and Tyler would ever really be past everything.

"Water under the bridge, babe..." Tyler said, smiling.

Epilogue

"Kash?" Jet queried, knocking lightly on Kashena's office door.

"Come on in, Jet," Kashena said, smiling.

Jet walked into the office, noting the blond with the black roots sitting there. She had an interesting biker chick look to her. Jet thought she looked vaguely familiar.

"Jet, this is Lyric Falco," Kashena said, gesturing to the woman. "Lyric, this is Jet Mathews, she's my best informant development asset," she said, winking at Jet.

Lyric's sky-blue eyes sparkled as she extended her hand to Jet. "Good to meet you," Lyric said, her smile warm.

"Lyric has come to us asking for some help," Kashena told Jet. "She's working with the AG's human trafficking task force, and she's hoping we can help out with some informant information if we have any."

Jet nodded, her mind already running through her list, thinking about what would relate.

Lyric's cell phone rang at that point.

"Damnit," Lyric said, grinning, pulling out her phone and looking at the display. "Sorry, this is the wife, she's called twice, so I gotta take it, excuse me."

Kashena nodded, understanding all too well. Jet grinned.

Lyric picked up the call. "Hey honey, what's up?" she asked. She listened for a moment, and tried to subdue a grin, but apparently her wife could tell. "No, I swear I'm not smiling..." she said, quirking a grin at Jet and Kashena. "Babe... honey... babe... Savanna!" she finally said when she obviously wasn't going to get a word in edgewise. "You know Cody, she's gonna do what she wants anyway... I know, but honey, she's old enough now to make those decisions for herself... Okay, okay, what's she trying to buy? That's a Ninja, right? She's got a Ninja, why would she buy another one?" she asked then, rolling her eyes and shaking her head. "Okay, okay, wait, babe... It's how many?" Lyric gave a low whistle. "Nice..." Then she grimaced when apparently that got her into trouble. "No, I'm not saying... Honey... she's twenty-two, we really can't tell her she can't have it..." She rolled her eyes again. "Yeah, I can talk to her babe, but... I know, but... Yes, sometimes she listens to me, but... if... honey... babe... Savanna, you're killin' me right now, okay?" Lyric said, not looking too put out by the prospect.

Kashena and Jet watched the woman talk on the phone and easily sensing that she was very much in love with her wife, even when her wife was obviously being somewhat difficult.

"Okay, babe, send me the article on the Kawasaki, I'll read it, and talk to Cody later okay? No, she won't buy it without talking to me, you're right about that... Okay, send me the article. Okay, I love you too, I'll call you later."

Finally Lyric hung up the phone, looking over at Jet and Kashena and sensing that she was in company of 'family,' the gay community's term for other gays. "My wife gets a bit fanatical when our daughter is going off the rails a bit."

"Your daughter is Cody Falco?" Jet asked.

"Yeah," Lyric said, "you know her?"

"Uh," Jet said, grinning. "Yeah, we've, uh, met," she said, her tone attempting discretion.

"Don't worry, I know my kid is rather prolific with women," Lyric said, grinning.

"Well, more recently she was of aid to my partner's girlfriend," Kashena said. "So she's earned her stripes with us."

"What kind of bike is she looking at?" Jet asked, having gathered enough from the conversation to ask.

"It's a new one, Kawasaki ZX-10R, a new version of a Ninja, but apparently it's pretty fast, two hundred and seven horsepower. You know bikes?" Lyric asked.

"Yeah," Jet said, nodding. "Some anyway. I'm actually selling my Ducati right now."

Lyric looked shocked. "What model?"

"Superleggera," Jet said, grinning. "Think your daughter would be interested?"

"Why would you sell a Leggera? And no, my kid doesn't have that kind of money..."

"Well, I'm looking to buy something my wife can ride with me on. Leggera's really aren't designed for passengers, ya know?"

"Man, I'd love to get my hands on a Leggera," Lyric said, shaking her head ruefully. "But the wife would kill me..." Then she gave Jet a sideways glance. "How much you selling it for?"

Jet tilted her head, pursing her lips. "Cop to cop, I'd sell it for forty-five k."

Lyric looked back at her stunned. "How old?"

"'Bout two years," Jet said.

"That's a sixty-five thousand dollar bike, how can you afford to lose that much?" Lyric asked, so shocked, she wasn't worried about sounding rude.

Jet laughed, glancing at Kashena. "Don't worry, I'm good."

Lyric looked considering. "Would you consider a trade?"

"What do ya got?" Jet asked, raising a black eyebrow.

"I have a custom Indian Roadmaster, worth about forty thousand, or I have a Harley Ultra Limited Low worth about thirty five, I'd give ya the difference... That is if the wife would buy off on it."

Jet considered the offer, nodding. "I'd have to see the bikes, and test them, but it's definitely not out of the realm of possibilities..."

Lyric, grinned, nodding. "My wife will likely be kicking me out tonight, but we'll just see what we see."

"So, getting back to this," Kashena said, grinning.

"Oh, shit, sorry," Lyric said, grimacing.

"No worries," Kashena said. "I have a Chief Deputy Attorney General for a wife, I get the hazards."

"At the AG's office?" Lyric asked. "Who?"

"Sierra Youngblood-Marshal," Kashena said.

Lyric looked surprised, but nodded. "Never would have guessed that one," she said, grinning. "But great lady, she kicks ass in a courtroom."

Kashena nodded, grinning. "Yeah, Sierra's pretty stealth, and a damned good lawyer too," she said.

Lyric nodded. "Anyway, I'm trying to see about getting some informants in the area of these gangs that are running girls, we're getting a lot of reports of gangs crossing enemy lines and joining forces, and it's not a good thing. We're noticing a serious uptick in prostitution and white slavery rings and the child porn market is booming, a lot of fresh meat. We gotta get a handle on it, and it was suggested that your unit might be of help."

Jet nodded. "I can definitely start tapping some of my sources, and also develop some new ones if you want to give me some ideas of what areas to work…" Jet said.

"You speak Spanish?" Lyric asked.

"And German, French, Arabic and some Farsi, why?" Jet said.

Lyric blinked a couple of times, surprised by the list Jet rattled off.

"She does that, it's annoying," Kashena said, grinning.

"You really speak all of those?" Lyric asked.

Jet nodded, not looking too impressed with herself. "I was thinking about learning Russian, how's that trade going?"

Lyric gave a short laugh. "As soon as you learn it call me, I got a few Russians I need to have some good conversations with."

Jet grinned, nodding. "Okay, so Mexicans, who?"

"The ESR in North East LA, and the BTLs in Central LA…" Lyric said.

Jet nodded. "Yeah, I can see what I've got… I think I might have a way in. Give me a week or so, okay?"

Lyric looked shocked, but nodded. "That would be incredible," she said nodding.

Jet took out a business card and wrote her cell number on the back, handing it to Lyric.

"Call me if you want to check out the Ducati," she said, grinning.

"That's just mean…" Lyric said, grinning too.

That evening Lyric walked into a heated discussion between her wife and their twenty-two year old daughter, Cody.

"Mom, its street legal!" Cody was insisting.

"I don't care, Cody, you don't need a bike with that much power, you'll get yourself killed!" Savanna was saying her light cocoa colored eyes flashing.

"Okay, okay, easy in here…" Lyric said, setting down her gear bag, and moving to kiss her wife's lips.

Lyric looked over at Cody, still not used to the green in her hair or the makeup she wore.

"You," she said, pointing at Cody. "Go take a shower, you're freaking me out with that shit," she said, gesturing to Cody's face and hair. "And you," she said, looking at Savanna, "come upstairs with me, I want to show you something…"

"Where have I heard that one before?" Cody said, grinning.

Lyric smacked her daughter on the butt. "Smart ass!"

Then she took her wife's hand, leading her upstairs to their master suite. Closing the door behind them, Lyric turned to Savanna, pulling her close and kissing her deeply. Savanna moaned softly, pressing against Lyric's five foot eight frame.

"Not fair," she murmured against Lyric's lips.

"All's fair babe…" Lyric murmured in reply.

They kissed for a few minutes, simply enjoying being close and in each other's arms.

"Okay, okay," Savanna said, finally forcing herself away from Lyric's lips. "What are you buttering me up for?"

Lyric grinned. "Okay, hear me out…" she said, which immediately had Savanna's eyes rolling. "Now stop that…" Lyric said, grinning wider. "I have a chance to buy a sixty-five thousand dollar bike for forty-five…"

Savanna gave Lyric a *really?* look. "I called you to get you to talk Cody *out* of buying another bike, how did it result in you wanting another one?"

"Well, when you called I was in a meeting…" Lyric said. "And it just so happened one of the people I was meeting with heard the conversation and is selling a Ducati Superleggera…"

"Oh Jesus," Savanna said. "Why does that sound really, really fast?"

"Because it's really, really fast…" Lyric said, smiling with her blue eyes sparkling in excitement.

"Don't smile at me like that…" Savanna said, looking heavenward as if asking for strength.

"Like what?" Lyric asked, her smile seemingly growing brighter.

"Like that, damn it Lyric!" Savanna said, biting her lip. "You know I can't resist you when you do that…" she said, sighing. "And it's damned unfair of you to do it to me…"

Lyric shrugged. "Hey, babe, a girl's gotta use what she's got…"

"And you have that damned perfect smile with those damnable blue eyes of yours..." Savanna said, crossing her arms in front of her chest. "What are you going to give up to buy the Leggera?"

"All business," Lyric said, winking. "I like that in a woman."

"Keep talking," Savanna said, her tone sassy now. "Or you'll be giving up both the Indian and the Harley..."

"But then you won't be able to ride with me babe..." Lyric said, her tone convincing.

"Maybe I'll learn to ride myself," Savanna said, her tone haughty.

"And maybe Elvis isn't really dead..." Lyric muttered.

"I heard that!" Savanna said, grinning.

It was true, Savanna wasn't likely to learn to ride a motorcycle. She didn't like all the extra work needed to ride a bike. She much more enjoyed holding on to Lyric as she did the hard work, plus it was a nice feeling to ride behind her wife.

"I said it loud enough for you to hear that, babe," Lyric said, grinning.

"So which one?" Savanna said.

"Dunno, I offered either of them, it would be up to Jet."

"Jet?" Savanna repeated.

"Yeah, that's her name," Lyric said.

"Interesting," Savanna said, nodding.

"Well?" Lyric asked her tone quizzical.

"You know I always have a hard time saying no to you," Savanna said.

"I know," Lyric said, smiling fondly.

"But you always ask me," Savanna said, putting her hand to Lyric's cheek. "And that's what I love about you."

"That I always ask?" Lyric queried.

"That you always think enough of me to ask," Savanna replied.

"Always babe," Lyric said. "Always."

In her own master suite in her mothers' house, Cody took a shower, washing off the makeup and washing her hair to get the green color out of it. Her hair was white blond with the black roots, like Lyric's. Unlike Lyric's longer hair, Cody wore it in a sort of long fade, the top longer, with shaved sides and back. Cody then focused on washing her body, with the soap skimming over the tattoo on her thigh, the letters SUR. A slight grimace flickered quickly across her face. Gritting her teeth she continued her shower.

Lyric found Cody later in the backyard, smoking and drinking a Smirnoff Ice. She was tossing balls for her two pit bulls, rescues from the local shelter. Lyric grinned; this was Cody's way of dealing with things, she'd take in strays to fix them. Lyric and Savanna had insisted she limit it to two dogs at a time, but Cody was forever getting them to the point of being so sweet that she easily adopted them out and was able to go back and adopt more. The local shelter loved her for that. Cody focused on pit bulls, saying, "Nobody wants them, I know how that feels."

"So, Mom says you want a new bike…" Lyric said, moving to sit across from her daughter.

Cody nodded. "And she thinks it's too fast."

"She does," Lyric said.

"And what do you think?" Cody asked, her hazel eyes looking over at Lyric, expressionless.

"I think that you're gonna do what you want to do anyway," Lyric said. "But that's not a bike you can afford to lay down," she said, shaking her head slowly. "So you'd damned well better be careful, or there won't be any skin left for a skin graft. You got me?"

Cody pressed her lips together seriously, nodding.

"Your mother loves you, so do I. We just don't want you to get hurt, Code," Lyric said, knowing that even though Cody wasn't her biological child, Cody was just like her at that age; wild and itching to push the envelope to the max.

"I know, Mom," Cody said. "But sometimes I just gotta go fast…"

"The demons'll still be there, Code, 'cause they're in here," Lyric said, leaning forward touching the center of Cody's chest.

Cody nodded, looking circumspect.

"Just be safe," Lyric said then, knowing that Cody would take in what she wanted and discard what she didn't want to hear or feel.

Lyric went into the house a few minutes later, and she and Savanna both heard Cody's phone playing music. Savanna looked sharply over at Lyric when she heard the song they heard far too often. The song, "Crawling" by Linkin Park, had lyrics sent chills up Savanna's spine every time she heard their daughter listening to it. What was worse, was that Cody always sang the words with conviction. Lyric stepped over to Savanna, hugging her as the song played outside. The lyrics talked about wounds that wouldn't heal and that it was so hard to control how she was feeling. They were very dark, very deep lyrics and spoke to all of Cody's inner demons.

"I hate that damned song…" Savanna gritted out, as the song ended.

"I know, babe," Lyric said, rubbing Savanna's back. "We can't fix everything. You of all people know that."

"It doesn't make it any easier to take," Savanna sighed.

"I know," Lyric said, glancing out the kitchen window at their headstrong daughter, knowing that Cody had a long way to go. "She'll get there, babe."

"Before or after she manages to kill herself?" Savanna asked.

Lyric looked back at her wife, grimacing and shaking her head. "I wish I knew."

They both stared out the kitchen window, watching Cody play with the dogs and both hoping that she could work through a short but traumatic lifetime of issues. They would be there for her every step, but there were some steps they couldn't take for her…

Also in the WeHo series:

When Love Wins

When Angels Fall

Break in the Storm

Turning Tables

Marking Time

Jet Blue